"I reckon I'm still waiting for the right woman to come along."

"Think you'll ever find her?" April asked.

Reed leaned close. "Oh, I found the right woman a long time ago. But I'm still waiting for her to come around to my terms."

April's heart thumped hard against her ribs. Her hands trembled so much, she had to hold on to one of the mugs in front of her. "What…what are your terms, Reed?"

His voice whispered with a rawhide scrape against her ear. "I only have one stipulation actually. I want that woman to love me with all her heart. I want her to love me, only me, enough to stay by my side for a lifetime and beyond."

April looked up at him then and saw the love there in his stalking cat eyes—the love and the challenge. "You don't ask for much, do you, cowboy?"

Books by Lenora Worth

Love Inspired

The Wedding Quilt #12
Logan's Child #26
*I'll Be Home for
  Christmas* #44
Wedding at Wildwood #53
His Brother's Wife #82
Ben's Bundle of Joy #99
The Reluctant Hero #108
One Golden Christmas #122
*When Love Came to Town #142

*Something Beautiful #169
*Lacey's Retreat #184
**The Carpenter's Wife #211
**Heart of Stone #227
**A Tender Touch #269
†A Certain Hope #311

*In the Garden
**Sunset Island
†Texas Hearts

Steeple Hill

After the Storm #8

LENORA WORTH

grew up in a small Georgia town and decided in the fourth grade that she wanted to be a writer. But first, she married her high school sweetheart, then moved to Atlanta, Georgia. Taking care of their baby daughter at home while her husband worked at night, Lenora discovered the world of romance novels and knew that's what she wanted to write. And so she began.

A few years later, the family settled in Shreveport, Louisiana, where Lenora continued to write while working as a marketing assistant. After the birth of her second child, a boy, she decided to pursue her dream full-time. In 1993, Lenora's hard work and determination finally paid off with that first sale.

"I never gave up, and I believe my faith in God helped get me through the rough times when I doubted myself," Lenora says. "Each time I start a new book, I say a prayer, asking God to give me the strength and direction to put the words to paper. That's why I'm so thrilled to be a part of Steeple Hill's Love Inspired line, where I can combine my faith in God with my love of romance. It's the best combination."

A CERTAIN HOPE

LENORA WORTH

Steeple
Hill®

Published by Steeple Hill Books™

STEEPLE HILL BOOKS

Steeple
Hill®

ISBN 0-373-81225-6

A CERTAIN HOPE

Copyright © 2005 by Lenora H. Nazworth

All rights reserved. Except for use in any review, the reproduction
or utilization of this work in whole or in part in any form by any
electronic, mechanical or other means, now known or hereafter
invented, including xerography, photocopying and recording, or in
any information storage or retrieval system, is forbidden without
the written permission of the editorial office, Steeple Hill Books,
233 Broadway, New York, NY 10279 U.S.A.

All characters in this book have no existence outside the imagination of
the author and have no relation whatsoever to anyone bearing the same
name or names. They are not even distantly inspired by any individual
known or unknown to the author, and all incidents are pure invention.

This edition published by arrangement with Steeple Hill Books.

® and TM are trademarks of Steeple Hill Books, used under license.
Trademarks indicated with ® are registered in the United States Patent
and Trademark Office, the Canadian Trade Marks Office and in other
countries.

www.SteepleHill.com

Printed in U.S.A.

Now faith is the substance of things hoped for, the evidence of things not seen.
—*Hebrews* 11:1

To the Ricks family—
Barbara, Bob and especially Jordan.
You all hold a special place in my heart.

Chapter One

You've got mail.

Summer Maxwell motioned to her cousin Autumn as she opened the letter in her computer. "Hey, it's from April."

Autumn hurried over to the teakwood desk by the window. The Manhattan skyline was etched in sun-dappled shades of steel and gray in front of them as together they read the latest e-mail from their cousin and roommate, April Maxwell.

I'm at work, but I'll be leaving for the airport in a few minutes. I'm so nervous. I'm worried about Daddy, of course. And I'm worried about seeing Reed again. What if he hates me? Never mind, we all know he does hate me. Please say prayers for my sweet daddy, and for safe travel. And that my BMW makes it there ahead of me in one piece.

"That's our April," Summer said, smiling, her blue eyes flashing. "Her prayer requests are always so practical."

"Especially when they come to that car of hers," Autumn said through the wisp of auburn bangs hanging in her eyes. "She's not so worried about the car, though, I think. She's got a lot more to deal with right now, and that's her way of dealing with it. She's not telling us the whole story."

Summer tapped out a reply.

We're here, sugar. And we will say lots of prayers for Uncle Stuart. Tell him we love him so much. Keep in touch. Oh, and let us know how things go with Reed, too. He doesn't hate you. He's just angry with you. Maybe it's time for him to get over it already.

Summer signed off, then spun around in her chair to send her cousin a concerned look. "Of course, he's been angry with her for about six years now."

Reed Garrison brought his prancing gray-and-black-spotted Appaloosa to a skidding stop as a sleek black sports car zoomed up the long drive and shifted into Park.

"Steady, Jericho," Reed said as he patted the gelding's long neck. He held the reins tight as he walked the horse up to the sprawling stone-and-wood ranch house. "I'm just as anxious as you, boy," he told the fidgeting animal. "Let's go find out who's visiting Mr. Maxwell on this fine spring day."

Reed watched from his vantage point at

the fence as a woman stepped out of the expensive two-seater convertible. But not just any woman, oh, no. This one was very different.

And suddenly very familiar.

Reed squinted in the late-afternoon sun, then sat back to take a huff of breath as he took in the sight of her.

April Maxwell.

It had been six long years since he'd seen her. Six years of torment and determination. Torment because he couldn't forget her, determination because he had tried to do that very thing.

But April was, as ever, unforgettable.

And now she looked every bit the city girl she had become since she'd bolted and moved from the small town of Paris, Texas, to the big city of New York, New York, to take up residence with her two cousins, Summer and Autumn. Those three Maxwell cousins had a tight bond, each having been named for the seasons they were born in, each having been raised by close-knit relatives scattered all over east Texas, and each having enough ambition to want to get out of Texas right after finishing college to head east and seek their fortunes. Not that they needed any fortunes. They were all three blue-blooded Texas heiresses, born in the land of oil and cattle with silver spoons in their pretty little mouths. But that hadn't been enough for those three belles, no sir. They'd wanted to take on the Big Apple. And they had, each finding satisfying work in their respective career choices. They now roomed together in Manhattan, or so he'd been told.

He hadn't asked about April much, and Stuart Maxwell wasn't the type of man to offer up much information. Stuart was a private man, and Reed was a silent man. It worked great for both of them while they each pined away for April.

Reed walked his horse closer, his nostrils flaring right along with Jericho's, as he tested the wind for her perfume. He smelled it right away, and the memories assaulted him like soft magnolia petals on a warm summer night. April always smelled like a lily garden, all floral and sweet.

Only Reed knew she was anything but sweet.

Help me, Lord, he thought now as he watched her raise her head and glance around. She spotted him—he saw it in the way she held herself slightly at a distance—but she just stood there in her black short-sleeved dress and matching tall-heeled black sandals, as if she were posing for a magazine spread. She wore black sunglasses and a black-and-white floral scarf that wrapped like a slinky collar around her neck and head. It gave her the mysterious look of a foreign film star.

But then, she'd always been a bit foreign and mysterious to Reed. Even when they'd been so close, so in love, April had somehow managed to hold part of herself aloof. Away from him.

With one elegant tug, she removed the scarf and tossed it onto the red leather seat of the convertible, then ran a hand through her short, dark, tousled curls. With slow, deliberate steps he was sure she'd learned during her debutante years, she did a long-legged walk across the driveway, toward the horse and man.

"Hello, Reed."

"April." He tipped his hat, then set it back on his head, ignoring the way her silky, cultured voice moved like rich honey down his nerve endings. "I heard you might be coming home."

Heard, and lost more sleep than he wanted to think about right now.

"Yes," she said, her hand reaching out to pat Jericho's muzzle. "I drove from the Dallas airport."

"Nice rental car."

"It's not a rental. It's mine. I had it shipped ahead so I'd have a way to get around while I'm here."

Reed didn't bother to remind her that

they had several available modes of transportation on the Big M Ranch, from horses to trucks and four-wheelers to Stuart Maxwell's well-tuned Cadillac. "Of course. You always did demand the best." And I wasn't good enough, he reminded himself.

"I like driving my own car," she said, unapologetic and unrepentant as she flipped a wrist full of black-and-white shiny bangle bracelets. They matched to perfection the looped black-and-white earrings she wore. "I hope that won't be a problem for you."

"Not my problem at all," Reed retorted, his gaze moving over her, a longing gnawing his heart in spite of the tight set of his jaw. "Looks like city life agrees with you."

"I love New York and I enjoy my work at Satire," she said with a wide smile that only illuminated her big, pouty red lips. Then she glanced around. "But I have to admit I've missed this ranch."

"Your daddy's missed you," Reed said,

his tone going low, all hostility leaving his mind now. "He's real sick, April."

She lifted her sunglasses. "I know. I've talked to the doctors on a daily basis for the last two weeks."

In spite of her defensive tone, he saw the worry coloring her chocolate-brown eyes and instantly regretted the reason she'd had to come home. But then, he had a lot of regrets. "Seeing you will perk him up, I'm sure."

She nodded, looked around at the house. "Nothing has changed, and yet, everything is changing."

"You've been gone a long time."

"I've been back for holidays and vacations. Never saw you around much." The questioning look in her eyes was full of dare and accusation.

But he wouldn't give her the satisfaction of knowing he'd deliberately made himself scarce whenever he'd heard she was coming home to visit. Until now. Now he didn't have a choice. He couldn't run. Her daddy needed him here.

He shrugged, looking out over the roping arena across the pasture. "I like to go skiing for the winter holidays, fishing and camping during the spring and summer."

"Still the outdoorsman." She shot him a long, cool look. "That explains your constant absences."

"That and the fact that I bought up some of the land around here and I stay pretty busy with my own farming and ranching."

"You bought up Maxwell land," she said, her chin lifting in that stubborn way he remembered so well.

"Your daddy was selling, and I was in the market to buy."

She looked down at the ground, her fancy sandal toeing a clog of dirt just off the driveway. "He wouldn't want anybody else on this land. I'm glad you bought it."

For a minute, she looked like the young girl Reed had fallen in love with. From kindergarten on, he'd loved her—at first from a distance, and then, up close. For a minute, she looked as vulnerable and lonely as he felt right now.

But that passed. Like a light cloud full of hope and sunlight, the look was gone as fast as it had come. When she looked up at him, the coolness was back in her dark eyes. "I expect you to take care of this land, Reed. I know I can count on you to do that, at least."

"Thanks," he said, and meant it, in spite of the accusing tone in her last words. "You know I'd never do anything to hurt your daddy. He taught me a lot and he's given me a lot—me and my entire family, for that matter."

"Y'all have been a part of this land for as long as I can remember," she responded, her eyes wide and dark as she stared up at him.

Reed wondered if she was remembering their times together. He wondered if she remembered the way he remembered, with regret and longing and a bitterness that never went away, no matter how sweet the memories.

"I'll be right here, as long as Stu needs me," he told her. He would honor that promise, in spite of having to be near her again. He owed her father that much.

"I guess I'd better go on inside then," she said, her tone husky and quiet. "I dread this."

"Want me to go in with you?" Reed asked, then silently reprimanded himself for offering. He wouldn't fall back into his old ways. Not this time.

"No. I have to do this. I mean, he called me home for a reason, and I have to accept that reason."

Reed heard the crush of emotion in her voice and, whether out of habit or sympathy, his heart lurched forward, toward her. "It's tough, seeing him so frail. Just brace yourself."

"Okay." She nodded, turned and walked back by the stone steps to the long wraparound porch, headed for her car. Then she turned back, her shiny gamine curls lifting in the soft breeze. "Will we see you at supper?"

"Probably not." He couldn't find the strength to share a meal with her, not tonight.

"Guess I'll see you later then."

"Yeah, later."

Reed watched from across the fence as she lifted a black leather tote from the car, her every step as elegant and dainty as any fashion plate he'd seen on the evening news. But then, April Maxwell herself was often seen on the evening news. She worked at one of the major design houses in the country—in the world, probably. Reed didn't know much about haute couture, but he did know a lot of things about April Maxwell.

His mother and sisters went on and on about how Satire was all the rage both on the runways and on the designer ready-to-wear racks, whatever that meant. April was largely responsible for that, they had explained. Apparently, she'd made a good career out of combining public relations and fashion.

She was just a bit shallow and misguided in the love and family department. She'd given up both to seek fame and fortune in the big city.

And he'd stayed here, broke and heartbroken, to mend the fences she'd left behind. Well, he wasn't broke anymore. And he wasn't so very heartbroken, either.

Why, then, did his heart hurt so much at the very sight of her?

She hurt all over.

April opened the massive wooden double doors to her childhood home, her heart beating with a fast rhythm from seeing Reed again. He looked better than ever, tall and muscular, his honey-brown hair long on his neck, his hazel-colored cat eyes still unreadable. Reed was a cowboy, born and bred. He was like this land, solid and wise, unyielding and rooted. After all this time, he still had the power to get to her. And she still had regrets she couldn't even face.

Before she could delve into those regrets, she heard footsteps coming across
the cool brick-tiled entryway, then a peal
of laughter.

"Ah, *niña,* you are home, *sí?*"

April turned to find one of her favorite
people in the world standing there with a
grin splitting his aged face.

"*Sí,* Horaz, I'm home. *¿Como está?*"

"I'm good, very good," Horaz said, bob-
bing his head, his thick salt-and-pepper
hair not moving an inch.

"And Flora? How is she?"

"Flora is fine, just fine. She is cooking
up all of your favorites."

"That sounds great," April said, hugging
the old man in a warm embrace, the scent
of spicy food wafting around them. She
wasn't hungry, but she'd have to hide that
from Horaz and Flora Costello. They had
been with her family since her father and
mother had been married more than thirty
years ago. And after her mother's death
when April was in high school, they'd

stayed on to take care of her and her father. She loved them both like family and often visited with their three grown children and their families whenever she came home, which was rare these days. The entire Costello clan lived on Maxwell land, in homes they'd built themselves, with help from her father.

"You look tired, *niña*," Horaz said. "Do you want to rest before supper? Your room is ready."

April thought of the light, airy room on the second floor, the room with the frilly curtains and wide, paned windows that allowed a dramatic view of the surrounding pasture land and the river beyond. "No, I don't want to rest right now. I want…I want to see my father."

Horaz looked down at the floor. "I will take you to him. Then I will instruct Tomás to bring in the rest of your bags."

"Yes, I left them in the trunk of the car." She handed him the keys. "And how is Tomás? Does he like high school?"

"He's on the football team," Horaz said, grinning again. "My grandson scored two touchdowns in the final big game last fall. We won the championship."

"I'm glad to hear it," April said, remembering her own days of cheerleading and watching Reed play. He'd been a star quarterback in high school and had gone on to play college ball. Then he'd gotten injured in his senior year at Southern Methodist University. After graduating, he had come home to Paris to make a living as a rancher. She had gone on to better things.

Not so much better, she reminded herself. You gave up Reed for your life in New York. Why now, of all times, did she have to feel such regrets for making that decision?

"Come," Horaz said, taking her by the arm to guide her toward the back of the rambling, high-ceilinged house.

As they passed the stairs, April took in the vast paneled-and-stucco walls of the massive den to the right. The stone fireplace covered most of the far wall, a row of woven baskets adorning the ledge high over it. On the back wall, over a long brown leather couch grouped with two matching comfortable chairs and ottomans, hung a portrait of the Big M's sweeping pastures with the glistening Red River beyond. Her mother had painted it. The paned doors on either side of the fireplace were thrown open to the porch, a cool afternoon breeze moving through them to bring in the scent of the just-blooming potted geraniums and the centuries-old climbing roses.

As they neared the rear of the house, April felt the cool breeze turn into a chill and the scent of spring flowers change to the scent of antiseptics and medicine. It was dark down this hall, dark and full of shadows. She shuddered as Horaz guided her to the big master bedroom where the wraparound porch continued on each side, where another huge fireplace dominated one wall, where her mother's Southwestern-motif paintings hung on either side of the room, and where, in a big bed hand-made of heart-of-pine posts and an intricate, lacy wrought-iron headboard that reached to the ceiling, her father lay dying.

Chapter Two

The big room was dark, the ceiling-to-floor windows shuttered and covered with the sheer golden drapery April remembered so well. When her mother was alive, those windows had always been open to the sun and the wind. But her mother was gone, as was the warmth of this room.

It was cold and dark now, a sickroom. The wheelchair in the corner spoke of that sickness, as did the many bottles of pills sitting on the cluttered bedside table. The bed had been rigged with a contraption that helped her weak, frail father get up and down.

April walked toward the bed, willing herself to be cheerful and upbeat, even though her heart was stabbing with claw-like tenacity against her chest. I won't cry, she told herself, lifting her chin in stubborn defiance, her breeding and decorum that of generations of strong Maxwell women.

"Daddy?" she called as she neared the big bed in the corner. "It's me, Daddy. April."

A thin, withered hand reached out into the muted light. "Is that my girl?"

April felt the hot tears at the back of her eyes. Pushing and fighting at them, she took a deep breath and stepped to the bedside, Horaz hovering near in case she needed him. "Yes, I'm here. I made it home."

"Celia." The whispered name brought a smile to his face. "I knew you'd come back to me."

April gasped and brought a hand to her mouth. He thought she was her mother! Swallowing the lump in her throat, she said, "No, Daddy. It's April. April…"

Horaz touched her arm. "He doesn't always recognize people these days. He has grown worse over the last week."

April couldn't stop the tears then. "I…I'm here now, Daddy. It's April. I'm April."

Her thin father, once a big, strapping man, lifted his drooping eyes and looked straight into her face. For a minute, recognition seemed to clarify things for him. "April, sweetheart. When'd you get home?"

"I just now arrived," she said, sniffing back tears as she briskly wiped her face. "I should have been here sooner, Daddy."

He waved his hand in the air, then let it fall down on the blue blanket. "No matter. You're here now. Got to make things right. You and Reed. Don't leave too soon."

"What?" April leaned forward, touching his warm brow. "I'm not going anywhere, I promise. I'm going to stay right here until you're well again."

He smiled, then closed his eyes. "I won't be well again, honey."

"Yes, you will," she said, but in her heart

she knew he was right. Her father was dying. She knew it now, even though she'd tried to deny it since the day the family doctor had called and told her Stuart Maxwell had taken a turn for the worse. The years of drinking and smoking had finally taken their toll on her tough-skinned father. His lungs and liver were completely destroyed by disease and abuse. And it was too late to fix them now.

Too late to fix so many things.

April sat with her father until the sun slipped behind the treeline to the west. She sat and held his hand, speaking to him softly at times about her life in New York, about how she enjoyed living with Summer and Autumn in their loft apartment in Tribeca. About how much she appreciated his allowing her to have wings, his understanding that she needed to be out on her own in order to see how precious it was to have a place to call home.

Stuart slept through most of her confessions and revelations. But every now and then, he would smile or frown; every now and then he would squeeze her fingers in his, some of the old strength seeming to pour through his tired old veins.

April sat and cried silently as she remembered how beautiful her mother had been. Her parents had been so in love, so perfectly matched. The rancher oilman and the beautiful, dark-haired free-spirited artist. Her father had come from generations of tough Texas oilmen, larger-than-life men who ruled their empires with steely determination and macho power. Her mother had come from a long line of Hispanic nobility, a line that traced its roots from Texas all the way back to Mexico City. They'd met when Stuart had gone to Santa Fe to buy horses. He'd come home with several beautiful Criollo working horses, and one very fiery beauty who was also a temperamental artist.

In spite of her mother's temper and artistic eccentricities, it had been a match made in heaven—until the day her mother had boarded their private jet for a gallery opening in Santa Fe. The jet had crashed just after takeoff from the small regional airport a few miles up the road. There were no survivors.

No survivors. Her father had died that day, too, April decided. His vibrant, hard-living spirit had died. He'd always been a rounder, but her devout mother had kept his wild streak at bay for many years. That ended the day they buried Celia Maxwell.

And now, as April looked at the skeletal man lying in this bed, she knew her father had drunk himself to an early grave so he could be with her mother.

"Don't leave me, Daddy," April whispered, tears again brimming in her eyes.

Then she remembered the day six years ago that Stuart had told his daughter the same thing. "Don't leave me, sugar. Stay here with your tired old daddy. I won't have anyone left if you go."

But then he'd laughed and told her to get going. "There's a big ol' world out there and I reckon you need to see it. But just re-member where home is."

So she'd gone on to New York, too eager to start her new career and be with her cousins to see that her father was lonely. Too caught up in her own dreams to see that Reed and her daddy both wanted her to stay.

I lost them both, she thought now. I lost them both. And now, I'll be the one left all alone.

As dusk turned into night, April sat and cried for all that she had given up, her prayers seeming hollow and unheeded as she listened to her father's shallow breath-ing and confused whispers.

Reed found her there by the bed at around midnight. Horaz had called him, concerned for April's well-being.

"Mr. Reed, I'm sorry to wake you so late, but you need to come to the hacienda right away. Miss April, she won't come out of his room. She is very tired, but she stays. I tell her a nurse is here to sit, but she refuses to leave the room."

She's still stubborn, Reed thought as he walked into the dark room, his eyes adjusting to the dim glow from a night-light in the bathroom. Still stubborn, still proud, and hurting right now, he reminded himself. He'd have to use some gentle persuasion.

"April," he said, his voice a low whisper.

At first he thought she might be asleep, the way she was sitting with her head back against the blue-and-gold-patterned brocade wing chair. But at the sound of his voice, she raised her head, her eyes widening at the sight of him standing there over her.

"What's the matter?" she asked, confusion warring with daring in her eyes.

"Horaz called me. He's worried about you. He said you didn't eat supper."

"I'm not hungry," she responded, her eyes going to her sleeping father.

"Okay." He stood silent for a few minutes, then said, "The nurse is waiting. She has to check his pulse and administer his medication."

"She can do that around me."

"Yes, she can, but she also sits with him through the night. That's her job. And she's ready to relieve you."

April whirled then, her eyes flaring hot and dark in the muted light from the other room. "No, that's *my* job. That should have been my job all along, but I didn't take it on, did I? I…I stayed away, when I should have been here—"

"That's it," Reed said, hauling her to her feet with two gentle hands on her arms. "You need a break."

"No," she replied, pulling away. "I'm fine."

"You need something to eat and a good night's sleep," he said, his tone soft but firm.

"You don't have the right to tell me what I need," she reminded him, her words clipped and breathless.

"No, I don't. But we've got enough on our hands around here without you falling sick on us, too," he reminded her. "Did you come home to help or to wallow in self-pity?"

She tried to slap him, but Reed could see she was so exhausted that it had mostly been for show. Without a word, he lifted her up into his arms and stomped out of the room, motioning with his head for the hovering nurse to go in and do her duty.

"Put me down," April said, the words echoing out over the still, dark house as she struggled against Reed's grip.

"I will, in the kitchen, where Flora left you some soup and bread. And you will eat it."

"Still bossing me around," she retorted, her eyes flashing. But as he moved through the big house with her, she stopped struggling. Her head fell against the cotton of his T-shirt, causing Reed to pull in a sharp breath. She felt so warm, so soft, so vulnerable there against him, that he wanted to sit down and hold her tight forever.

Instead, he dropped her in a comfortable, puffy-cushioned chair in the breakfast room, then told her, "Stay."

She did, dropping her head on the glass-topped table, her hands in her hair.

"I'm going to heat your soup."

"I can't eat."

"You need to try."

She didn't argue with that, thankfully.

Soon he had a nice bowl of tortilla soup in front of her, along with a tall glass of Flora's famous spiced tea and some corn bread.

Reed sat down at the table, his own tea full of ice and lemon. "Eat."

She glared over at him, but picked up the spoon and took a few sips of soup. Reed broke off some of the tender corn bread and handed it to her. "Chew this."

April took the crusty bread and nibbled at it, then dropped it on her plate. "I'm done."

"You eat like a bird."

"I *can't* eat," she said, the words dropping between them. "I can't—"

"You can't bear to see him like that? Well, welcome to the club. I've watched him wasting away for the last year now. And I feel just as helpless as you do."

She didn't answer, but he saw the glistening of tears trailing down her face.

Letting out a breath of regret, Reed went on one knee beside her chair, his hand reaching up to her face to wipe at tears. "I'm sorry, April. Sorry you have to see him like this. But…he wants to die at home. And he wanted you to be here."

She bobbed her head, leaning against his hand until Reed gave in and pulled her into his arms. Falling on both knees, he held her as she cried there at the table.

Held her, and condemned himself for doing so.

Because he'd missed holding her. Missed her so much.

And because he knew this was a mistake.

But right now, he also knew they both needed someone to hold.

"It's hard to believe my mother's been dead twelve years," April said later. After she'd cried and cried, Reed had tried to lighten things by telling her he was getting a crick in his neck, holding her in such an awkward position, him on his knees with her leaning down from her chair.

They had moved to the den and were now sitting on the buttery-soft leather couch, staring into the light of a single candle burning in a huge crystal hurricane lamp on the coffee table.

Reed nodded. "It's also hard to believe that each of those years brought your father down a little bit more. It was like watching granite start to break and fall away."

"Granite isn't supposed to break," she said as she leaned her head back against the cushiony couch, her voice sounding raw and husky from crying.

"Exactly." Reed propped his booted foot on the hammered metal of the massive table. "But he did break. He just never got over losing her."

"And then I left him, too."

As much as he wanted to condemn her for that, Reed didn't think it would be kind or wise to knock her when she was already so down on herself. "Don't go blaming yourself," he said. "You did what you'd always dreamed of doing. Stuart was—is—so proud of you. You should be proud of your success."

"I am proud," she said, her laughter brittle. "So very proud. I knew he was lonely when I left, Reed. But I was too selfish to admit that."

"He never expected you to sacrifice your life for his, April. Not the way I expected things from you."

"But he needed me here. Even though she'd been dead for years, he was still grieving for my mother. He never stopped grieving. And now…it's too late for me to help him."

"You're here now," Reed said, his own bitterness causing the statement to sound harsh in the silent house.

April turned to stare over at him. "How do you feel about my being back?"

Her directness caught him off guard. Reed could be direct himself when things warranted the truth. But he wasn't ready to tell her exactly how being with her made him feel. He wasn't so sure about that himself.

"It's good to have you here?" he said in the form of a question, a twisted smile making it sound lightweight.

"Don't sound so convincing," she said, grimacing. "I know you'd rather be anywhere else tonight than sitting here with me."

"You're wrong on that account," he told her, being honest about that, at least. "You need someone here. This is going to be tough and I...I promised your daddy I'd see you through it."

That brought her up off the couch. "So you're only here as a favor to my father? Out of some sense of duty and sympathy?"

"Aren't those good reasons—to be helping out a friend?"

"Friend?" She paced toward the empty fireplace, then stood staring out into the starlit night. "Am I still your friend, Reed?"

He got up to come and stand beside her. "Honestly, I don't know what you are to me—I mean, we haven't communicated in a very long time, on any level. I just know that Stuart Maxwell is like a second father to me and because of that, I will be here to help in whatever way I can. And yes, I'd like to think that we can at least be friends again."

"But you're only my friend because you promised my father?"

"Since when did this go from the real issue—a man dying—to being all about you and your feelings?"

"I know what the real issue is," she said, her words stony and raw with emotion. "But since you practically admitted you're doing this only out of the goodness of your heart," she countered, turning to stalk toward the hallway, "I just want you to know I don't expect anything from you. So don't do me any favors, okay? You're usually away when I come home. You don't have to babysit me. I'll get through this somehow."

"I'm sure you will," he said, hurt down to his boots by her harsh words and completely unreasonable stance. But then he reminded himself she was going through a lot of guilt and stress right now. It figured she'd lash out at the first person to try to help her, especially if that person was an old flame. "Guess it's time for me to get on home."

"Yes, it's late. I'm going to check on Daddy, then I'm going to bed." She started for the stairs, but turned at the first step, her dark head down. "Reed?"

He had a hand on the ornate doorknob. "What?"

"I do appreciate your coming by. I feel better now, having eaten a bit." She let out a sigh that sounded very close to a sob. "And...thanks for the shoulder. It's been a long time since I've cried like that."

He didn't dare look at her. "I'm glad then that I came. Call if you need anything else."

"I will, thanks." Then she looked up at him. "And I'm sorry about what I said. About you not doing me any favors. It was mean, considering you came here in the middle of the night just to help out. That was exactly what I needed tonight."

Reed felt his heart tug toward her again, as if it might burst out of his chest with longing and joy. He wanted to tell her that he needed her, too, not just as friend, but as a man who'd never stopped loving her.

Instead, he tipped his head and gave her a long look.

"I'll be here, April. I'll always be right here. Just remember that."

Chapter Three

April pressed the send button on the computer in her father's study, glad that she had someone to talk to about her worries and frustrations. Then she reread the message she'd just sent.

Hi, girls. Well, my first night home was a bad one. Daddy is very sick. I don't think he will last much longer. I sat with him for a long time—well into the night. Then Reed came in and made me eat something. Okay, he actually carried me, caveman-style, into the kitchen. Still Mr. Know-It-All-Tough-Guy. Still good-looking. And still single, from everything I can tell, in spite of all those rumors we've heard about his social life. He was very kind to me. He held me while I cried. And I cried like a baby. It felt good to be in his arms again. But I have to put all that aside. I have to help Daddy, something I should have been doing all along. Today, Reed and I are taking a ride out over the ranch, to see what needs to be done. I hope I can remember how to sit a horse. Love y'all. Keep the prayers coming. April.

That didn't sound too bad, she thought as she took another sip of the rich coffee Flora had brought to her earlier. She'd told Summer and Autumn the truth, without going into the details.

Oh, but such details.

After the devastation of seeing her father so sick, April hadn't wanted to go on herself. But Reed had made her feel so safe, so comforted last night. That wasn't good. She was very weak right now, both in body and spirit. Too weak to resist his beautiful smile and warm golden eyes. Too weak to keep her hands out of that thick golden-brown too-long hair. Too weak to resist her favorite cowboy. The only cowboy she'd ever loved.

You're just too emotional right now, she reminded herself. You can't mistake kindness and sympathy for something else— something that can never be.

Yet, she longed for that something else. It had hit her as hard as seeing her father again, this feeling of emptiness and need, this sense of not being complete.

Thinking back on all the men she'd met and dated in New York, April groaned. Her last relationship had been a disaster. All this time, she'd thought she just hadn't found the right one. But now she could see she was always comparing them to Reed.

That had to stop. But how could she turn

off these emotions when she'd probably see him every day? Did she even *want* to deny it—this feeling of being safe again, this feeling of being back home in his arms?

No, she wouldn't deny her feelings for Reed, but right now, she couldn't give in to them, either. They had parted all those years ago with a bitter edge between them. And he'd told her he wouldn't wait for her.

But he was still here.

He's not here because of you, she reminded herself. He's here because he loves your daddy as much as you do.

She couldn't depend on Reed too much. She had to get through this one day at a time, as her mother used to tell her whenever April was facing some sort of challenge.

"One day at a time," April said aloud as she closed down the computer. But how many days would she have to watch her father suffering like this?

"Give me strength, Lord," she said aloud, her eyes closed to the pain and the fear. *"Give me strength to accept that with*

life comes death. Show me how to cope, show me how to carry on. Please, Lord, show me that certain hope my mother used to talk about. That hope for eternal life."

Turning her thoughts to her father, April got up to take her empty coffee mug into the kitchen. She wanted to watch to see how the nurse fed him, so she could help. She wanted to spend the morning with him before she went for that ride with Reed. Actually, she didn't want to leave her father's side. Maybe she could stall Reed.

He'd called about an hour ago, asking if she wanted to check out the property. Caught off guard, and longing for a good long ride, April had said yes. Then she'd immediately gone to check on her father, only to find the nurse bathing him. April had offered to help, but the other woman had shooed her out of the room. At the time, a good long ride had sounded better than having to see her father suffer such indignities. But now she was having second thoughts.

"Finished?" Flora asked, her smile as bright as her vivid green eyes. Flora wore her dark red hair in a chignon caught up with an elaborate silver filigree clip.

April put her mug in the sink, then turned. "Yes, and thanks for the Danish and coffee. You still make the best breads and dainties in the world, Flora."

"Gracias," Flora said, wiping her slender hands on a sunflower-etched dish towel.

"And how you manage to stay so slim is beyond me," April continued as she headed toward the archway leading back to the central hall.

"Me, I walk it all off, but you? You need to eat more pastry," Flora said, a hint of impishness in her words.

April turned to grin at her, her eyes taking in the way the morning sunlight fell across the red-tiled counters and high archways of the huge kitchen. Even later in the year, in the heat of summer, this kitchen would always be cool and tranquil. She'd spent many hours here with her mother and Flora, baking cookies and making bread.

"I guess I walk mine off, too." April shrugged, thinking how different life on the ranch was from the fast pace of New York. Here, she could walk for miles and miles and never see another living soul, whereas New York was always full of people in a hurry to get somewhere. Wanting to bring back some of the good memories she had of growing up here, she said, "Maybe I'll make some of that jalapeño bread. Remember how Daddy used to love it?"

"*Sí,*" Flora said, nodding. "He can't eat it now, though, *querida.*"

"Of course not," April said, her mood shifting as reality hit her with the same force as the sunbeam streaming through the arched windows. "I'm going to talk to the nurse to see what he can eat."

Flora nodded, her brown eyes turning misty with worry. "He is a very sick man. I keep him in my prayers."

"I appreciate that," April said. "I guess our only prayer now is that God brings him some sort of peace, even if that means we have to let him go."

"You are a very wise young woman."

"Mother taught me to trust in God in all things. I'm trying to remember that now more than ever."

"Your *madre,* she loved the Lord."

"Yes, she did," April said. Then she turned back to the hallway, wishing that she had the same strong faith her mother had possessed. And wishing her father hadn't ruined his health by drinking and smoking.

As she entered his room, she heard him fussing with the nurse. "I don't…need that. What I need… is a drink." Stuart's eyes closed as he fell back down on the pillow and seemed to go to sleep again.

The nurse, a sturdy woman with clipped gray hair named Lynette Proctor, clicked her tongue and turned to stare at April. "Man can barely speak, and he still wants a drink." She gave April a sympathetic look. "His liver is shot, honey. Whatever you do, don't give him any alcohol."

"I don't plan on it," April retorted, the woman's blunt words causing a burning anger to move through April's system. "And I'd like to remind you that this man is my father. You will show him respect, no matter how much you agree or disagree with his drinking problem."

Lynette finished administering Stuart's medication, checked his IV, then turned with her hands on her hips to face April. "I apologize, sugar. My husband was an alcoholic, too, so I've seen the worst of this disease. That's one reason I became a nurse and a sitter. I feel for your daddy there, but I just wish…well, I wish there was something to be done, is all."

"We can agree on that," April said, her defensive stance softening. Then she came to stand over the bed. In the light of day, her father looked even more pale and sickly. "This isn't the man I remember. My daddy was so big and strong. I thought he could protect me from anything."

"Now it's your turn to protect him, I reckon," Lynette said. "Do you still want to go over his schedule?"

"Yes," April said. "Show me everything. I'm going to be here for the duration." She stopped, willing herself to keep it together. "However long that might be."

Lynette touched a hand to her arm. "Not as long as you might think, honey. This man ain't got much more time on this earth. And I'm sorry for your pain."

"Thank you," April said, wondering how many times she'd have to hear that from well-meaning people over the course of the next weeks. *How much can I bear, Lord?*

Then she remembered her mother's words to her long ago. *The Lord never gives us more than we can bear, April. Trust in Him and you will get through any situation, no matter the outcome.*

No matter the outcome. The outcome here wasn't going to be happy or pretty.

Her father was dying. How could she bear to go through that kind of pain yet again?

She turned as footsteps echoed down the hallway, and saw the silhouette of a tall man coming toward her.

Reed.

He'd said he'd be around for the duration, too.

April let out a breath of relief, glad that he was here. She needed him. Her father needed him. Maybe Reed's quiet, determined strength would help her to stay strong.

No matter the outcome.

Reed listened as the very capable Lynette told them both what to expect over the next few weeks. It would get worse, she assured them. He might go quietly in his sleep, or he might suffer a heart attack or stroke. All they could do was keep him comfortable and out of pain.

With each word, told in such clinical detail, Reed could see April's face growing paler and more distressed. He had to get her away from this sickroom for a while, because he knew there could be many more days such as this, where she could only sit and watch her father slipping away.

When Lynette was finished, Reed motioned to April. "He's resting now. Good time to take that ride."

At the concern in her dark eyes, he whispered, "I won't keep you out long. And Lynette can radio us—I have a set of walkie-talkies I bought for that very reason."

"I'll take my cell phone," April replied, watching her father closely. Then she turned to Lynette and gave her the number. "Call me if there is any change, good or bad."

"Okay," Lynette said. "He'll sleep most of the afternoon. He usually gets restless around sundown."

"We'll be back long before then," Reed said, more to reassure April then to report to the nurse.

Seeming satisfied, April kissed her father on the forehead and turned to leave the room. Once they were outside in the hallway, she looked over at Reed. "I don't think I should leave him."

He understood her fears, but he also understood she needed some fresh air. "A short ride will do you good. It'll settle your nerves."

"Just along the river, then."

"Whatever you say. You're the boss."

April shot him a harsh look. "Don't say that. I'm not ready to be the boss."

"Well, that's something we need to discuss," Reed replied. "A lot of people depend on this land for their livelihoods." He hesitated, looking down at the floor. "And...well, Stu let some things slip."

"What do you mean, let some things slip?"

"Fences need mending. We're got calves to work and brand. Half our hands have left because Stu would forget to pay 'em. Either that, or he'd lose his temper and fire 'em on the spot."

April closed her eyes, as if she was trying to imagine her father roaring at the help. Stuart had a temper, but he'd always handled his employees with respect and decency. When he was sober, at least.

"You keep saying 'our' as if you still work here."

Reed placed his hands on his hips, then raised his eyes to meet hers. "I've been helping out some in my spare time."

Groaning, she ran a hand through her bangs. "Reed, you have almost as much land now as we do. Are you telling me you've been working your ranch and this one, too? That's close to fifteen hundred acres."

"Yeah, pretty much. But hey, I don't really have anything better to do. Daddy helps, too. And you know Stu's got friends all over East Texas. Your uncles come around as often as they can, to check on things and help out. Well, Richard does—not so much James. But they have their own obligations. We've all tried to hold things together for him, April."

She let out a shuddering breath. "I'm just not ready for all of this."

"All the more reason to take things one day at a time and get yourself readjusted."

"There's no way to adjust to losing both your parents," she said. Then she hurried up the hallway ahead of him, the scent of her floral perfume lingering to remind him that she was back home, good or bad.

Reed watched as April handled the gentle roan mare with an expert hand. "I see you haven't lost your touch."

April gave him a tight smile. "Well, since you told Tomás to bring me the most gentle horse in the stable, I'd say I'm doing okay."

"Daisy needed to stretch her legs," he replied.

"I still go horseback riding now and then."

"In New York City?"

She laughed at his exaggerated way of saying that. "Yes, in New York City. You can take the girl out of the country—"

"But you can't take the country out of the girl?"

"I guess not." She urged Daisy through the gates leading out to the open pasture. "Who's that other kid with Tomás?" she asked as the two teenagers waved to them from where they were exercising some of the other horses.

"That's Adan Garcia. They're best friends and they play football together. He helps Tomás with some of the work around here. Just a summer job."

"Why is he staring at us?" she asked. "He looks so bitter and…full of teenage angst."

Reed shrugged. "Guess he's never seen a woman from New York City before. Maybe that ain't angst, just curiosity about a 'city girl.'"

"Will you please stop saying that as if it's distasteful?"

"Not distasteful. Just hard to imagine."

"You never thought I'd make it, did you?"

"Oh, I knew you'd give it your best."

She kneed Daisy into action, tossing him a glare over her shoulder.

Reed followed on Jericho, anxious to know everything about her life since she'd been gone. "So what's it like in the big city?"

She clicked her boots against Daisy's ribs as they did a slow trot. "It's exciting, of course. Fast-paced. Hectic."

"Your eyes light up when you say that."

"I love it. I enjoy my work at Satire and it's fun living with Summer and Autumn."

Reed turned his head to roll his eyes. What kind of name was Satire, anyway? But right now, he didn't need to hear about her fancy threads workplace. So he asked the question that had been burning through his system since she'd come home. No, since she'd left. "And how about your social life? Dating any Wall Street hotshots or do you just hang with the Hollywood types?"

She slanted him a sideways look. "Honestly, I rarely have time to date."

His gut hurt, thinking about all the eligible bachelors in New York. "I don't believe that."

"Okay, I've had a few relationships. But...I've found most of the men I date are a bit self-centered and shallow. They're so involved in their careers, they kind of rush their way through any after-hours social life. I don't like to be rushed."

That made him grin. In his mind, she'd just described herself. Her new self. But then, maybe he'd misjudged her. "You never did like to be rushed. Maybe the city hasn't changed you so much after all."

"No, I haven't changed that much. I know where I came from. And besides, most of my colleagues tease me about my Texas drawl."

Reed could listen to that drawl all day long. "You have that edge in your voice now. That little bit of hurried city-speak."

"City-speak?" She grinned. "I can't imagine what you're talking about."

"Oh, you know. Fast and sassy."

As they walked the horses toward the

meandering river, she gazed out over the flat grassland. Red clovers and lush bluebonnets were beginning to bloom here and there across some of the pastures. "Well, fast and sassy won't cut it here, unless I'm roping cattle. But at least I can apply my business skills to detangling some of the mess this ranch is in."

"How long do you plan on staying?"

Her eyes went dark at that question. "I...I told my supervisor I'd be here indefinitely. I have three weeks of vacation time and she agreed to let me use my two weeks of sick days. I've never abused my benefits at Satire, so she knew I was serious when I came to her asking for an extended leave of absence."

"And when...things change here, you'll go back?"

"That's the plan."

Reed didn't respond to that. But his silence must have alerted April.

Pulling up, she turned to stare over at him from underneath her bangs. "You do understand I have to go back?"

He nodded, pushed his hat back on his head. "I understand plenty. But tell that to your daddy. He has other plans, I think."

She shook her head. "I'm not even sure he realizes I'm here."

"Oh, he knows. It's all he's talked about for the last week. Every time he'd wake up, he'd ask for you. I kept telling him you were on your way. I think he's been waiting for you to get home just so—"

She looked cornered, uncertain. "Just so what? What do you mean? That he's going to give up and die now? After seeing him, I've accepted that, Reed."

"Yeah, well, that's something we can't help, but there's more to it."

Her eyes widened with fear and confusion. "Why don't you just explain everything, then? Just give me the whole story."

Reed didn't want to have to be the one to tell her this, but somebody had to. Stu had revealed it in his ramblings and whispered words. And Reed had promised the

dying man he'd see it happen. "April—
your father—he thinks you've come home
for good."

Chapter Four

"Home for good?"

April stared over at Reed, a stunned wave of disbelief coursing through her system.

Reed nodded, looked out over the flowing river. "He has it in his head that you'll just take over things here. I mean, it's all going to be yours, anyway. It's in his will. And Richard and James both know that."

"My uncles have agreed to this?"

"They'll get their parts—a percentage of the oil holdings and mineral rights, things like that. But for the most part, the land and the house will belong to you."

April swallowed the pain that scratched at her throat. "I thought…I just figured he'd delegate things to Uncle James and Uncle Richard. I thought I'd get only my mother's part of the estate." She shuddered, causing Daisy to go into a prance. "Honestly, Reed, I've tried not to think about that at all."

"Well, start thinking," he said, the words echoing out over the still pasture. Then he waved a hand in the air, gesturing out over the landscape. "Pretty soon, all of this will be yours, April. And that means you'll have a big responsibility. And some big decisions."

She didn't want to deal with this today. "Could I just get settled and—could I concentrate on my father, just for today, Reed? I'll worry about all of that when the time comes."

"Okay," he replied, his tone as soft as the cooing mourning dove she could hear off in the cottonwood trees. "I won't press you on this, but I just thought you should know."

"I'm not sure what I'll do," she admitted. "I just don't know—"

"We'll work through it," he said, a steely resolve in his words.

"You don't have to help me, Reed." She could tell he didn't want to be tied down to the obligations her father had thrust onto his shoulders. And neither did she.

"I don't mind," he said, turning to face her as he held the big Appaloosa in check.

"Well, maybe I do," she retorted.

And because she felt herself being closed in, because she felt as if she were back in college and Reed was telling her what was best for her all over again, she spurred Daisy into a fast run and left Reed sitting there staring after her. She had to think, needed to feel the spring wind on her face. This was too much to comprehend all at once.

Way too much for her to comprehend. Especially with Reed sending her those mixed messages of duty and friendship. She didn't want his pity or his guidance if it meant he was being forced to endure her.

She could handle anything but that. So she took off.

Again.

Reed caught up with her at the bend in the river where a copse of oak saplings jutted out over a broken ridge. Just like April to take off running. She'd always run away when things got too complicated. She was doing the same thing now that she used to do whenever they'd fought. She'd get on her horse and take off to the wild blue yonder. Sometimes she'd stay gone for hours on end, upsetting her parents and the whole ranch in general with her reckless need to be away from any kind of commitment or responsibility.

Well, now she was going to have to stop running.

"April," he called as he brought Jericho to a slow trot beside her. "Slow down and let's talk."

"I don't want to talk," she said over her shoulder.

But she slowed Daisy anyway. Even April wouldn't run a poor horse to the grave.

Reed pulled up beside her as they both brought the horses to a walk. "Let's sit a spell here by the water. Then we'll head back and I'll point out some of the most urgent problems around here."

"I think I know what the most urgent problem is," she retorted as she swung off Daisy. "My father is dying."

Reed allowed her that observation. He knew all of this had to be overwhelming. He hopped off Jericho and stepped over to take Daisy's reins. "I understand how you must be feeling, April. That's why I'm here to help."

She turned on him, her brown eyes burning with anger and hurt. "But you don't want to be here. I can see that. I don't want you to feel obligated—"

Reed tugged her close, his own anger simmering to a near boil. "You don't get it, do you? I *am* obligated. To your father, and to you. What kind of man would I be if I just walked away when you both need me?"

"You mean, the way I walked away,

Reed? Why don't you just go ahead and say it? I walked away when my father needed me the most. I was selfish and self-centered and only thought of myself, right?"

He nodded, causing her to gasp in surprise. "I reckon that about sums things up," he said. "But if you aim to keep on punishing yourself, if you aim to keep wallowing in the past and all that self-pity, then maybe you don't need me around after all. You seem pretty good at doing that all on your own. That and running away all over again."

He handed her Daisy's reins and turned to get back on Jericho, to wash his hands of trying to be her friend. He could just concentrate on being nearby when the time came. He could hover around, checking on things, without having to endure the double-edged pain of seeing her and knowing she'd be gone again soon.

"Reed, wait."

He was already in the saddle. It would be

so easy to just keep going. But he didn't. He turned Jericho around and looked down at April, his heart bolting and bucking like a green pony about to be broken. Just like his heart was about to be broken all over again.

"I don't want to fight you, April. I just want to help you." He shrugged. "I mean, don't we have that left between us at least? When a friend needs help, I'm there. It's just the way it is."

She stared up at him, her brown eyes soft with a misty kind of regret, her short curls wind-tossed and wispy around her oval face. She was slender and sure in her jeans and T-shirt, her boots hand-tooled and well-worn.

"It's just the way *you* are, Reed," she acknowledged with her own shrug. But her eyes held something more than the regret he could clearly see. They held respect and admiration and, maybe, a distant longing.

He still loved her. So much.

"I need…I do need your help," she admitted. "I don't think I can handle this on my own. You were here when my mother died. Remember?"

"I remember," he said, nodding. He remembered holding April while she cried, right here on this spot of earth, in this very place, underneath the cottonwoods by the river. They'd watched the sun set and the stars rise. They'd watched a perfect full moon settle over the night sky. And he'd held her still. Held her close and tight and promised her he'd never, ever leave her.

Would he be able to keep that promise this time?

Reed knew he could keep his promises. But he also knew April hadn't learned how to do the same.

But he got down off his horse and took her hand anyway. He didn't dare hope. He didn't dare think past just holding her hand. "I'll be right here," he told her.

"Thank you." She smiled and took his hand in hers, a tentative beginning to a new truce.

* * *

They stayed there, in what used to be their special spot, for about an hour. April had called the house twice to check on her father, so Reed decided maybe he'd better get her home. At least he'd been able to fill her in on some of the daily problems around the ranch. They'd somehow made a silent agreement to concentrate on business. Nothing personal.

"How about we head back?" Reed asked now. April seemed more relaxed, even though he could tell she was concerned over this latest news of her becoming full owner of the Big M. "I'll show you the backside of the property. Should be home just in time for vittles."

That made her laugh at least. "You truly will always be a cowboy, won't you, Reed?"

He nodded, flipping his worn Stetson back on his head. "I was born that way, ma'am."

She laughed again at the way he'd stretched out the polite statement. "I hear you bought one of our guest houses for yourself."

"Yep." He got back on Jericho, noting the animal was impatient to get moving again. "A right nice little place. Three bedrooms, two baths, oak floors, stone fireplace and a game room that begged for a new billiards table."

April slipped back on Daisy with ease. She always had been a grand horsewoman.

"I'm glad someone is occupying that house. It always seemed silly to me to send guests to another house when we have so much room in the big house."

"Ah, but that's the way of the Texas cattlemen. Showy and big. The bigger, the better in Texas."

They trotted along at a reasonable pace, back over the rambling hills of northeast Texas. Reed took in the dogwoods just blooming in the clumps of forest at the edge of the vast pastureland, their blossoms bright white amid the lush green of the sweet gums and hickory and oak trees. Here and there, rare lone mesquite trees jutted at twisted angles out in the pasture, like signposts pointing toward home.

"It's funny how small our apartment is in New York, compared to all this vast property," April said.

"I would have thought you'd feel stifled there amid all the skyscrapers and traffic jams," Reed said, then wondered why he'd even made the comparison.

"I did at first," she replied, the honesty in her eyes surprising him. "The city took some getting used to. But now…well, I like being a part of that pulse, that energy. In a way, New York is as wide-open and vast as this land. You just have to find the rhythm and go with it."

"Too fast-paced for me," Reed said, thinking they were straying back into personal territory. To lighten things, he asked, "How do Summer and Autumn like it?"

"They love it, too," April replied, laughing. "We all joke with our friends about how we left small towns with such big, famous names—Paris, Athens, and Atlanta—only to wind up in the biggest city of all—New York."

"I guess your friends do get a kick out of making fun of our slow, country ways."

"No, we don't allow that," she quickly retorted, an edge of pride in her tone. "Reed, you never did get that we loved our lives here in East Texas, but we all felt we had to get away, in order to...to become independent and sure-footed."

That statement had his skin itching, as if barn fleas had descended on him. "Seems you could have done that right here on the Big M."

"No, no, I couldn't," she said, giving him a slanted look. "I felt stifled *here,* Reed. I feel free in the city."

"Well, that just doesn't make a lick of sense, April."

"I know," she replied, her head down as Daisy picked her way over a bed of rocks and shrubs. "It's hard to explain, hard to reason, but Daddy depended on me so much. I couldn't replace my mother, Reed.

And I knew he'd never marry again. I had to get away."

Hearing the fear in her words, hearing that soft plea for understanding, Reed got it for the first time. April hadn't been running from him, necessarily. She'd been trying to spread her wings and get out from under the grief her father had carried in every cell of his being. "It must have been hard for you, having to see him that way, day in and day out."

"It was. So when Summer and Autumn jokingly suggested we all head east, I jumped at the chance. I was the one who convinced them to just try living in New York with me for a while."

He wanted to ask her why she'd turned to her cousins instead of him, the man she supposedly loved. But he guessed staying here with him would only have moved her from one dependent man to another. Maybe she was afraid because of what she'd seen happen to her father. Reed told himself he wouldn't have smothered her, but in his heart he knew he certainly would have cherished her, and he probably would have been overly protective.

Instead he only nodded. "New York— about as far away from East Texas as a body can get. And you've all been there ever since."

"Yes, although I think they'd both like to come home more than me, truth be told. They don't say that, but I've gotten hints that Summer has been thinking about that for a while. She had a very bad relationship end recently and I think she's longing for the safe structure of her hometown and her family. Or at least the structure her grandparents gave her, growing up."

"Why didn't she come home with you? She could visit Athens easily."

"Work. She's a counselor at our neighborhood YWCA in New York. She loves her work, but it's so easy to become burned out, dealing with inner-city families on a daily basis. Their lifestyles are sure different from what we're used to."

"I can only imagine," Reed replied. Then he asked a question that he hoped April wouldn't take the wrong way. "Do y'all have a church in New York?"

April quickly nodded. "Oh, yes. We all attend a lovely brownstone chapel not far from our apartment."

"I'm glad to know you kept the faith, even in big ol' New York City."

She gave him a measuring look. "Preaching to me, Reed Garrison?"

"No, just checking to make sure you haven't completely changed on me."

"I'll have you know there are lots of Christians in the big city."

"Glad to hear it."

She gentled Daisy to a slow walk. "Reed, I've never lost my faith in the Lord. Summer and Autumn and I all know that God is in control of all things. We don't hide our Christianity. We celebrate it. That's why Summer just broke things off with her boyfriend. He resented her faith, used it to taunt her. She wouldn't allow him to undermine something so important in her life. None of us would do that."

Reed nodded, sensing from her strong tone that maybe April had been through a similar situation. But he refused to ask her about that. "Summer always was the most sensitive of all of you."

"Yes, and Autumn is the most practical. Which leaves me, the shallow one, right?"

He turned to face her, then reached across to hold Daisy's rein. "I never said you were shallow, April. I might have thought that at one time, but now—"

"Maybe now you're finally seeing the real me, at last."

Reed was just about to comment on that and tell her that he'd like to get to know the real her, when suddenly Daisy whinnied and started kicking her front legs in the air. "Whoa, there, girl," Reed said, glad he still had a grip on the mare's reins.

"What on earth?" April said, settling the horse down with soothing words and a tight tug on the reins.

Reed dismounted and stared down at where Daisy had landed. "Glass," he said, shaking his head.

"Daisy must have stepped in it," April replied, hopping down to stand beside him. "Is she hurt?"

Reed calmed the animal, then stood facing Daisy. He moved his hands down the mare's front right leg to the fetlock, then leaned in to support the animal as he pulled Daisy's right front foot up. "Yep. Got a chunk of bottle glass embedded, right there." He pointed to a tender spot just inside Daisy's shoe. "No wonder she got spooked." Then he motioned toward Jericho. "I've got a farrier's knife in my saddle bag. If you don't mind getting it for me, I'll try to see if I can clean her foot at least."

April did as he asked, quickly finding the instrument and bringing it to Reed. She watched as he moved the knife around Daisy's hoof and shoe. As Reed worked, a rounded piece of thick gold-colored glass fell out from Daisy's hoof. "Looks like the chunk hit her right against the frog, then got stuck near the shoe. She's gonna be bruised for a few days."

"We need to get her home and let someone look at this."

Reed nodded his agreement. "I can put some duct tape over it for now. Then I'll call the vet."

April searched his saddlebag for the tape. "You travel prepared, Mr. Garrison."

"Yes, ma'am. You never know what you'll need out here alone. Have to take care of our horses."

April gave him a proud look. "I feel good, knowing you've been watching out for things around here. I'm sure my father appreciates it."

"Just doing my job," Reed replied, embarrassed and touched by her compliment. He'd jump through fire to help Stuart Maxwell. And his daughter.

"I guess we'd better walk her home," April said, patting Daisy on the nose. "It's gonna be okay, pretty girl."

Reed glanced around. "Looks like someone has been camping out here. And maybe drinking something stronger than a soda. They must have had a good time, breaking up all these empty bottles."

"Trespassers, just one more thing to worry about," April said. Then she glanced up at him. "I'll need to ride home with you."

Reed heard the hesitancy in her words. "Well, if you'd rather walk—"

"No, no. It's a long way. I don't mind riding shotgun."

His gazed moved over her face. "Are you sure?"

"Of course I'm sure. How many times have we ridden double over the years?"

Reed remembered those times. Too vividly. "Well, let's get going," he said, the edge to his voice making him sound curt. "We'll have to go slow for Daisy's sake."

When he had April settled behind him in the saddle, he tried to ignore the sweet smell of her hair and the way her hands automatically held to him. Instead, he concentrated on the mess they'd just left.

"We'll have to find out who's been having field parties out in our back pasture," he said over his shoulder. "Probably kids out for kicks."

"Yes," she answered, her tone so soft, Reed almost didn't hear it.

He had to wonder—was being this close causing her as much discomfort as it was him?

Discomfort and joy, all mixed up in the same confusing package. But then, that described his feelings for April exactly.

Lord, I need your help. I need to show restraint and self-control. Please help me to do and say the right things. Lord, just help me out here in any way you can.

The spring wind whipped across the open pasture in a gentle whispering, as if in answer to Reed's silently screaming prayers.

Chapter Five

❧

While Reed took care of Daisy's foot with a medical boot until the vet could get there, April immediately went to see her father. As she left the warm sunny day outside and waited for her eyes to adjust to the dark recesses of the back part of the house, she said a prayer for her father.

"Lord, he never...my father never went to church with my mother. Show him the way home, Lord. Don't let him go without accepting You into his heart."

Lynette Proctor stepped out of the bedroom. "Oh, I thought I heard a voice out here. Are you okay, honey?"

April looked at the husky nurse, wondering if she could trust the woman. "I was saying a prayer for my father."

"Oh, how sweet." Tears pricked at Lynette's brown eyes. "If it makes you feel any better, I read to him from the Bible every night. I don't know if he can hear me or not, but I read anyway. Helps to pass the time, and it sure can't hurt for both of us to get a lesson."

"I appreciate that," April replied. "And I'm sorry about yesterday."

Lynette ran a work-worn hand over her clipped gray hair. "What in the world are you talking about?"

"I was rather rude to you—"

"Think nothing of that, sugar. You wouldn't believe what I've seen. Death brings out a lot of emotions, both good and bad. And when it's like this, where we have to wait—well, I've seen catfights right over a dying soul, people arguing over the will already, things like that. Family is very important, but some families just don't realize what they've got until it's too late."

April looked into the darkened room. "We've only got each other, my father and I."

Lynette's big eyes widened. "Oh, I wouldn't say that. Your father has had a host of friends coming and going since word got out that he's in a bad way. They say a man can tell how rich he is by his friends. He might be dying, but he was a very wealthy man, friend-wise. He can't take all his millions with him, but he sure can take those kind words and the way his friends have held his hand and told him how much they love him. He can take that to his grave."

April felt hot tears filling her own eyes. "Thank you, Mrs. Proctor. That's very reassuring."

"Call me Lynette, honey." Then she pulled an envelope out of her pocket. Oh, I almost forgot. Flora told me to be sure and give you this."

April took the cream-colored envelope,

recognizing the fancy paper and the engraved address. "An invitation to the Cattle Baron's Ball. Daddy always loved this event when my mother was alive."

She thought back over the pasture full of longhorns she and Reed had seen while riding the land. The lanky herds of spotted cattle had milled around, getting fat off the bounty of the lush range, their droopy eyes and elegant long horns giving them a distinctive, sullen look. Reed had pointed out Old Bill, their senior sire bull, and several calves who'd been born recently. The Big M was famous for its quality, pure-bred longhorns. Just one more thing that tradition demanded of April. She'd have to keep that going long after her father was gone.

"I suppose I'll have to get used to attending such events," she said, wishing her father could guide her on what to do.

Lynette squinted at her. "Well, Flora said something about your attending in honor of your father."

April frowned and shook her head. "Oh, I couldn't. Not with Daddy so sick."

Lynette patted April's hand, then shrugged. "Just passing the message on. Flora really wanted you to have this. Maybe you should talk to her about it."

"I will," April said, rubbing a finger over the envelope. "And I'll send my regrets."

So many regrets, April thought as she went into her father's bedroom and sank down in the chair next to his bed. Stuart was sleeping, his breathing labored and irregular. The doctors had explained his condition, and how he would slowly deteriorate, but April still had a hard time accepting that the frail figure lying in this bed was her father.

"Hi, Daddy," she said, her voice squeaky and husky. "It's April. I went for a ride with Reed." She reached over to grasp her father's hand, noticing the bulging veins and the age spots covering his hand. "We have such a beautiful place here, Daddy." She looked at his hand and felt it move slightly. Maybe he could hear her. "I don't know what to do, Daddy. I'm not sure I'm up to the task of running the Big M. But I won't ever let it go, I promise. Somehow, I'll find a way. I promise you that."

Tears spilled from her eyes as she realized the implications of the promise she'd just made. Leaning over, April laid her head on her father's soft, clean-smelling cotton blanket. "Don't leave me, Daddy. If you'd only get well, I'd do anything. I know I left you once, when you begged me to stay. And now…it's too late to change that. But… if we just had one more chance."

Holding her father's hand tightly with both of hers, April sobbed, her grief and her regret so overwhelming that she didn't think she'd make it through the next few weeks.

Then she felt Stuart's hand moving beneath hers. Surprised, she raised her head. "Daddy?"

With a ragged effort, her father tugged his hand away from her grasp. Disappointment surged through April's system. Was he turning away from her pleas?

But Stuart didn't turn away. Instead, he opened his eyes and reached up to her face, his bony fingers trailing through her dark curls like wisps of smoke. "Love you, Sweet Pea," he managed to say, the words coming long and hard and labored. "Trust you." Then he dropped his hand and fell back asleep.

April stayed at his bedside, a smile on her face in spite of the tears she shed.

Reed sat at the big oak desk he'd bought from an antique store in Dallas. He'd put it in the roomiest of the extra bedrooms of what used to be the Big M guest house. This room had a view of the rolling green pastures and the well-stocked fish pond at the back of the property. He could see the big house from here, too. He could see the arched double window of April's upstairs bedroom, located right over the swimming pool. That window caused memories to come swirling back, like moondust caught in spiderwebs.

Maybe he was caught in a web, too. A web of need and longing for something that could never be. He turned to the big collie lying at his feet. "Well, Shep, old boy, she's back and I'm in big trouble. Any suggestions?"

Shep yawned, stretched his front paws across the Aztec-style rug covering the hardwood floor and grunted a reply.

"You're no help," Reed retorted. "No help at all."

The phone rang then, making Shep bark and Reed jump. "Man, I gotta get a grip."

"Reed, it's Richard Maxwell. I was just calling to check on things at the Big M."

"Hello, Richard," Reed said, glad to hear from Stuart's brother. "I guess you've heard April's home?"

"Yeah, the girls e-mail back and forth. They're pretty worried about her and Stu. How's she taking things?"

"Not too good. She's devastated about her father, of course. And she's not sure about the future."

"Who is, these days? How's my brother?"

Reed filled Richard Maxwell in, wondering why the man hadn't called April directly. But then, the Maxwell brothers had come to depend on Reed lately to give them the truth, straight-up, about the ranch and their brother. So Reed told Richard the truth. "I don't expect him to last much longer, Richard."

"We're making arrangements to come over," Richard told him. "I tracked James down and he and I hope to be there by the weekend. And I might tell the girls to come on down, too."

"That would be good. I know Summer and Autumn would be a big help to April. You know how close they all are."

"I sure do," Richard said, laughing. "Three peas in a pod, that's what we've always called them."

"It's hard on April, being here alone," Reed said.

"She's not alone, boy. She has you. You always could talk her down—and we all know how high-strung she can be at times."

"I hear that," Reed said, a smile creeping across his lips. "I'm just not sure I can be of much help—"

"You're solid, Reed," Richard replied.

"Stuart knows that. That's why he's set such high store in you."

"I appreciate the vote of confidence," Reed replied, not feeling confident at all.

They talked a few more minutes about the day-to-day operations of the ranch, then Richard said goodbye. Reed didn't mind that Stuart's brothers were keeping close tabs on things at the Big M. He wouldn't have it any other way. After all, a lot was at stake here. The livestock, the land, the oil leases, the acreage, the house and surrounding buildings—it all added up to a big amount of responsibility and a huge amount of revenue. But it was more than the wealth. The Big M was home. It always would be home.

At least, to Reed.

But would April want to make it home again?

That question nagged at Reed as he worked at his computer, filing away bills and keying in information on the spring calving season. It was a busy time, both for him personally, with his spot of land and his own growing herd, and for the Big M.

"I sure don't need any…"

Distractions. He was going to say distractions. But April Maxwell was much more than a distraction. She was like that piece of glass that had found its way into Daisy's foot. April was embedded inside Reed's heart. And he had the big bruise to prove it.

Reed sat, watching the sun set over the hills. He sat there and prayed for guidance and strength as he stared up at those windows—windows that shielded the woman he loved.

"Hi, girls."

April typed the greeting to her two cousins back in New York. She knew that they'd read the e-mail together, as they did each night when they all gathered around the computer, taking turns checking their personal messages, then sharing the really good ones with each other.

What would she do without Summer and Autumn? She was the oldest by two years, but her cousins were both very sensible and mature. Summer was more temperamental and subject to fiery outbursts of temper, while Autumn was always calm and in control. But they both felt the Maxwell loyalty just as much as April did. She had to wonder how different their lives might be if she hadn't dragged them to New York with her all those years ago.

Wishing they were both here, she continued her update.

Daddy is about the same today. But he did something so very sweet. I was talking to him, crying, wishing he'd just get up out of that bed. And he heard me! He touched his hand to my face and told me he loved me.

It was so special. My daddy never was one for words, you know. I don't remember the last time he said that to me. It took all of his effort, but now I know he has forgiven me for leaving him. I should have never done that. I love my life in New York with y'all, but now I'm wishing I'd just stayed here and worked somewhere closer to home—Dallas had a lot of potential. I knew that. Houston, even. Why did I have to go all the way across the country? Okay, I did it because Reed was pressing me to settle down. He got too close, too fast. I needed to be independent. I felt closed in by so much grief and pain. I guess I was afraid to let go of my heart after losing Mother. I can see that now. Funny how time causes us to look back and just all of a sudden see things so much more clearly.

I know what you're saying to each other—that it was our plan, our dream. We had to stick together. We had to show our formidable fathers that we could strike out on our own, just as they all had. Even now, all these years later, it's so hard to admit that we were all running from something.

We succeeded, but is it enough? Is it enough that I left Reed and my daddy behind? Is it enough that Summer had to go through that terrible relationship with Brad Parker in order to realize her real worth? Or that she still can't make a commitment to anyone because of how her parents left her on her grandmother's doorstep? Is it enough, Autumn, that you always have to have concrete proof of anything— that you can't go on faith alone, even in your love relationships, even in knowing that Summer and I love and support you, no matter what? No wonder none of us can find a man. We've set our sights way too high and we've forgotten what really matters. I guess all of this has got me thinking about things—how do we know we've made the right choices in life? Have we really listened for God's voice, or have we just listened to what we wanted, what we thought we needed, whether it hurt others or not?

I walked away from Daddy's grief and Reed's overbearing love. Summer, you've been turning to the wrong men all your life because you don't want to be abandoned ever again. And yet, they've all let you down, especially Brad. And Autumn, well, girl, you have to have too many details, too many charts and graphs in life. We all need to loosen up and turn back to the Lord. We need to go on faith and let it all work itself out.

Oh, I didn't mean to preach. Really I didn't. I'm just so confused right now. Did I tell y'all I went riding with Reed this morning? Did I tell y'all that I think I still love him?

I have to turn in soon, but I want to go and sit with Daddy for a while. Don't take what I said the wrong way, please. I'll be okay. We will always be okay, because we have each other. I wish y'all were here, but I know you have work to do—other obligations.

Other obligations kept me away from home for so long. Now, I have only one obligation. I have to get through watching my father die. Summer, maybe you should call Uncle James. He is your father, after all. Maybe you could make amends, make your peace with him. Before it's too late.

"Wow." Autumn Maxwell turned to her cousin after she finished reading the e-mail from April. "I've never heard April talk like that. She must really be depressed."

Summer shifted on the deep-cushioned red couch they'd found at a second-hand store in Soho. "Yeah, to even suggest I get in touch with my daddy. She's obviously not thinking very clearly. She knows where I stand on that issue."

"But…she's looking at it from a different angle now, honey. Uncle Stuart is dying. April's thinking your daddy, or even mine, could die, too. And with so much left unsaid."

Summer tossed back her long blond hair. "Some things are better left unsaid. You know that, Autumn."

"But I'm beginning to wonder if that philosophy is so wise," Autumn replied, hoping she sounded encouraging. "What would it hurt—"

Summer hopped off the couch, her black yoga pants dragging against her bare feet. "It would hurt *me,* so let's change the subject, please."

Autumn sent her cousin a questioning look, but all she got in return was Summer's retreating back and the slamming of her bedroom door.

Autumn sighed, and turned back to the computer.

Hi, April. I don't think Summer's ready for any sage advice just yet, sweetie. But I understand how you must be feeling. It must be so hard to watch your father die. I am sending you hugs and prayers. And I promise, if you just say the word, we will both come home, whether Summer wants to do so or not. She might not want to face her parents yet, but she will do anything to help you get through this. Promise.

Now, tell me all about your ride with Reed. I want details, good and bad. And I want to know the exact minute you realized you still loved him. I want to know what that must feel like. I've never been in love, you know. I have to live vicariously through you, I reckon.

So, tell me everything. Is Reed as goodlooking as ever? Or even better?

April had to laugh at her cousin's inquisitive nature. Autumn was all business during the day. She was a CPA at an exclusive Manhattan firm—a firm that her powerful father had managed to get her an interview with, an interview that Autumn had protested at first—that independence thing again. But Autumn had taken things from there and she'd fought hard to make her father proud. She worked long hours, as well as most weekends, and she barely had a social life. But Autumn said she liked things that way. April believed that Autumn secretly wanted to break loose and live a little, but she just didn't know how. Autumn was the quintessential good girl, right down to her oh-so-proper white cotton PJs. But Autumn was also a very good listener. Her cousin could be very precise in getting to the heart of a matter.

And right now, April's own heart was being torn apart by her father's sickness and the sure acceptance that she still loved Reed Garrison.

It's a long story, she typed. I hope you're not sleepy tonight. And yes, Reed is even more gorgeous than he was when I left him. He's mature and a bit weathered, but still very attractive.

And there's more. Daddy wants me to take over the Big M. On a permanent basis. That would mean I'd have to stay here. Near Reed. I don't know if I'm ready for that responsibility. I need advice, cousin. Good advice.

I don't know what to do.

April signed off the computer and stood up to look out the windows of her room. She looked toward the east. She could see the dark shape of the brick guest house Reed now lived in. It was so like Reed to buy a house that had a clear view of the Big M's main house. It was so like him to stand guard over this ranch.

She saw the light from a single lamp burning into the night, and she wondered if Reed was down there, looking up at her window. She wondered if he was thinking about her right now.

April turned from the window and crawled into the crisp, sweet-smelling sheets of her bed, secure in the warm feeling of knowing Reed was nearby.

Ever watchful.

He'd always been right here, waiting.

But how long could a man wait for a woman who was so frightened of giving her heart away?

Chapter Six

"Vandals?"

Reed nodded at his father's one-worded question.

"Yep. It's been happening a lot lately."

Sam Garrison held tightly to his stallion's reins, then glanced down at the left-over campfire. "Charred beer bottles. Cigarette butts. Kids, maybe?"

"Has to be," Reed responded, walking Jericho toward the broken fence wire near the main highway. "They must be sneaking in off the main road. Probably parking their cars in that clump of trees just around the curve to the Big M."

"How much damage have you found so far?" his father asked, squinting underneath his worn straw cowboy hat.

"April and I saw the same thing about two days ago, on our ride around the property near the river. Daisy got a sliver of glass from that little campfire. She's still bruised. Stepped on some broken, burned-out bottle glass. Now this. I'd say some of the locals are having field parties on Big M property."

"Did you ever do things like this when you were young, son?" Sam asked, a grin splitting his bronze-hued face.

"Did you?" Reed countered, his own grin wry. Then he shook his head. "I didn't have to trespass, remember? I was lucky enough to live on the Big M."

Sam tipped his hat at that comment. "And lucky enough to be just about the same age as the heir apparent."

"I don't recall mentioning April," Reed

said, his grin dying down into ashes, just like this campfire had.

"Didn't have to mention her. She's written all over your face."

"It shows that much?" Reed asked, dropping his head down in mock shame.

"Son, I'm not a rocket scientist," Sam said, "but your mama and I know you still love April. Your mother thinks that's why you've never found anyone else."

"In spite of Mom's efforts to hook me up with every single lady at church and beyond?"

"Yep. Your ma loves you and…well, she wants some grandchildren. So do I. You know, we ain't getting any younger."

"Look mighty fit and young to me," Reed said, hoping to sway the conversation away from April.

But he should have known better. His father was as shrewd as they came, a real cowboy poet of sorts, a literary man who could quote Emerson and Thoreau and could still ride a horse and herd cattle better than any other man on the Big M.

"I'm fit, all right," Sam replied, slapping a hand to his trim stomach. "But fit don't cut it when a man's wishing for the next generation to carry on."

"I'm carrying on for you just fine, I thought," Reed said, frowning.

"That you are. Working the Big M and your own place. Makes a man proud. But…you're kind of stubborn in the love department. You ought to go after that girl, show her that you were wrong all those years ago."

"Me?" Reed shouted the word so loudly, Jericho did a little prance of irritation. "Me?" he repeated with a low growl. "Maybe your memory is getting rusty, Daddy. April was the one who had to get away from this place and away from me. I couldn't very well hightail it to New York and kidnap her. I don't want a woman who won't come willing to me."

"Then make her *want* you, boy," his father said. "I had to do that with your mama."

"Oh, really. And here I thought she was the one who caught you."

"I let her think that, of course. But your mama was as prim and proper as they come. Still is. Had to woo her all kinds of ways. By the time I got through courting her, she was as strung up as a baby calf on branding day."

"Not a pretty picture, Pa," Reed said, shaking his head as he chuckled. "Don't think Mama would appreciate being compared to a calf."

"Well, she's certainly called me a stubborn old bull a few times," his father countered in a testy tone. Then he tilted his head. "Besides, we were talking about your love life, not mine. Mine's been just fine for close to thirty-five years."

Reed pinched his nose with two fingers, willing the tension in his head to go away. "Whereas mine is nonexistent, right?"

"Got that right, yes sir."

"Would you listen if I told you with the utmost respect to kindly stay out of my business?"

"Probably not." Sam waved his hand in frustration. "You need to get on with it or get over it, son."

"I'm trying," Reed said in a ground-out tone that made him sound more mad than he really was. "I'm trying."

Sam shook his hat and put it back on. "Tough times, these. Hard to watch one of my best friends dying right before my eyes. And one of the finest men in all of Texas, at that. Guess I shouldn't be pushing you back toward April. That girl's got enough to worry about without having you underfoot."

"That's why I'm trying to play it safe," Reed said, glad his father understood that at least. "I can't push her or rush her, Daddy. Not now, when she's so scared and hurt. I tried that the last time, and she bolted like a scared pony. She's…well, I've never considered April as fragile, but right now, that's exactly what she is. I don't want to be the one to break her."

Sam urged his horse forward. "Then be gentle, son. Show some understanding. You always did go in with guns blazing, in any situation. Might want to curve that domineering gene you obviously inherited from your ma's side of the family."

"Yeah, right," Reed said, smiling at his father. "You can blame it on Mom, but we both know you're as mulish and demanding as they come when you want to be."

"Who, me?" His father feigned innocence by rising his bushy brows and scrunching up his ruddy nose.

"Guess I got it double," Reed reasoned as he followed his father back toward home.

"You could say that," Sam agreed, his laughter echoing out over the pastures and trees.

Reed loved his parents with a fierceness that made his heart ache, and he loved what they had between them, that strong sense of loyalty and friendship that had been tempered by faith and family, through hard times and good times. He wanted that kind of love, that kind of commitment for himself.

And he wanted it with only one woman.

As they neared the lane leading back to the big house, Reed couldn't help but look up at that arched window. He hadn't talked to April today. He'd wanted to give her some time with her father. Time alone. Precious time. He'd wanted to give her so much, but he'd held back.

He was learning restraint, at long last. He was learning patience, at long last. He was learning what his wise father had been trying to tell him. That old cliché was true. Sometimes, in order to win back something you loved, you had to let it go. Well, he'd tried that route. And he'd learned to be patient the hard way through all those years. It hadn't brought April back. But she was back now, under sad circumstances. And this time, he wouldn't make any mistakes. He'd be patient, he'd be gentle, he'd be steady and sure. Reed wouldn't use her grief and despair to bring her back to him. That would be wrong, so wrong. But he'd be nearby if she needed him.

Lord, let it be right. Let it happen in your own good time, as Mama would tell me.

Grief was no way to start a relationship, or to bring April back to his way of thinking.

So he'd keep on waiting. And hoping. It was the only thing he could do.

Laura Garrison busied herself with setting the table in the kitchen of the big house. April helped her, putting out silverware and tea glasses, glad for the quiet strength Reed's mother possessed.

"I'm so glad you came by," April said, remembering all the times Reed's mother had been a guiding force in her life, especially after April's own mother had died. "And I insist that you and Mr. Sam stay and help me eat all this food."

"I wouldn't mind visiting with you," Laura said, her big brown eyes lighting up. "That is, if you're up to company."

"I could use the company," April admitted. "I've spent all day with Daddy, reading to him, talking to him. Sometimes, he opens his eyes and…it's almost as if he's smiling up at me. Other times, he just sleeps."

Laura finished basting the baked chicken. "The rolls are almost ready," she said as she came to help April with the salad and vegetables. "I hate that you're having to go through this, sugar. Stuart has always been our rock, strong and steady, a good leader with a heart of gold."

"That heart is old and worn-out now," April said, her hands gripping the cool tiles of the counter. She'd sent Flora and Horaz back to their house to rest and enjoy their own dinner. They needed a good night's sleep and some peace and quiet. Sam Garrison was sitting with her father while she and Laura prepared dinner. "Everyone here is so devoted to him. That has brought me a lot of comfort."

"We all love your daddy," Laura said,

her shiny bob of brown hair flowing across her forehead with a defined slant. "And we all encouraged him to give up that bottle. But he just didn't have the strength. It's been hard on all of us. That's why I wanted to come and see you. We're all in this together, April."

April reached out to hug her friend. "Thank you so much. And please, stay for dinner and… why don't you call Reed, too? It'll do me good to have y'all for company. I can't stand the loneliness."

"Are you sure?" Laura asked.

April knew what she was asking. Did she really want Reed there?

"I'm sure." April nodded. "You don't have to walk on eggshells around me, Miss Laura. Reed and I, we've made a truce of sorts. Now is certainly not the time to bring up past hurts and regrets."

"*Do* you have regrets?" Laura asked, her eyes clear and full of understanding. Then she put a hand to her mouth. "I'm so sorry. I shouldn't have asked that."

"It's okay," April replied. "And the answer is yes. I regret that I was selfish enough to leave my father when he really needed me to stay. And I regret that I hurt Reed."

"You had to do what you thought best," Laura said with a shrug.

It was so like Reed's mom not to pass judgment. But April knew Laura Garrison loved her son first and foremost.

"I had to get away, yes," April said, hoping to explain. "I had to grow and expand my horizons, so to speak. But mostly, I knew I could never make Daddy happy. Not in the way my mother made him happy. And I've never admitted this, but I was so afraid I'd never be able to make Reed happy, either. I…I didn't think I could settle down and be a ranch wife. I'm not like you, Miss Laura."

Laura's chuckle surprised April. "Honey, do you really think any woman is prepared to be a ranch wife? It's a hard job. Being a wife and a mother are hard jobs, no matter where you live. But if you love someone enough—"

"You make sacrifices," April finished. "I wasn't ready for that sacrifice."

"Well, you know, Reed could have met you halfway."

April shook her head. "What? Should I have made him move to New York with me? I hardly think Reed would have been happy living in the big city."

"No," Laura agreed. "But he could have fought harder to…to try a long-distance relationship."

"It would never have worked," April replied, sure as rain that Reed would have been miserable. "I couldn't ask that of him."

"You never tried," Laura pointed out with a soft smile.

"I didn't want to force him to wait for me."

"Honey, he's still waiting," Laura said. "Think about that. And if I know my son, I think he'll keep on waiting, because he's not going to get between you and the grief you're feeling right now."

That revelation hit April with all the force of being thrown from a horse. *Was*

Reed truly still waiting for her? She'd wondered that so many times, had even hoped that might be the case. Then another thought even more formidable hit her.

Was she still waiting for Reed, too?

That question nagged at April all through dinner. Reed's parents were pleasant and upbeat, keeping the conversation light. They talked about the warm spring weather, about the alfalfa growing in the pastures, about the livestock moving through the fields and paddocks. They talked about April's job in New York and asked questions about life in the big city.

And while they talked, Reed sat silent and still, a soft smile flickering across his wide mouth now and then. He toyed with his tea glass and ate his chicken with the relish of a hearty appetite, his eyes settling now and then on April.

Each time he looked at her, something shifted and slipped inside her, like river water gliding over a rockbed. She thought back over the years she'd been away and wondered how she'd ever managed to leave him. Was it the grief eating away at her? Or was it the regret?

I have to be sure, Lord, she thought. *I have to be sure that if I decide to stay here and do my father's bidding, that it's for all the right reasons. I don't want to hurt Reed again. And I can't take any more hurt myself. Help me, Lord. What is Your will in all of this?*

"Ready for some dump cake?" Laura asked now.

"I'm always ready for cake," Sam replied, winking at April.

Laura got up, but Reed put a hand on his mother's arm.

"I'll get it, Mom. Coffee, too?"

"Sure," Laura said, the surprise in her voice sparkling through her eyes.

"Want to help me?" Reed asked April.

She glanced up at him, wondering what he was up to. But his eyes held only a warm regard that made her feel secure and safe. "Yes. I'll bring the coffee if you get the plates for the cake."

"I think we can handle that," Reed said. She saw the warning look he sent to his two curious parents. "You two behave while we're getting dessert."

"Us? We'll just sit here and let your ma's fine cooking settle while you young folks do the rest of the work," his father replied, his eyes twinkling.

"They are so cute together," April said, not knowing what else to say.

The laughter and whispers coming from the table across the arched, tiled kitchen washed over her like a familiar rain. She loved Reed's parents and had always wished her own parents could have had such a solid, stable, long-term relationship. Instead, Stuart and his Celia had had more of a roller-coaster ride of intense love and obsession, followed by bouts of anger and fire— Until death had ended it all, leaving both April and her father shocked and devastated.

She could see now that her mother's sudden death had been at the core of her fears. She was beginning to realize that maybe that was the main reason she'd been so afraid to give in to her love for Reed. That was why she'd run away. She couldn't deal with something so rich and intense just after losing her mother. What if she lost Reed, too?

You did lose him, she reminded herself as she gathered coffee cups and cream and sugar onto a long porcelain serving tray adorned with sunflowers and wheat designs.

"You look mighty serious there," Reed said over her shoulder, grabbing the coffee carafe before she could put it on the tray. "I'll take this over, then come back for the cake and plates."

April watched as he set the coffee carafe on the table. He had that long-stride walk of a cowboy, that laid-back easy stride of a man comfortable in his own skin.

And he looked good in that skin, too.

Stop it, she told herself as she looked away from Reed and back to the heavy mugs she'd put on the tray. When Reed came back to the counter, she looked up at him, then asked him in a low voice, "Why have you never married?"

From the look in his eyes, she wished immediately she could take that question back. But it was out there now, hovering over them like a swirl of dust, stifling and heavy.

If the question threw him as much as it had her, he hid it well behind a wry smile. But he didn't miss a beat in answering. "I reckon I'm still waiting for the right woman to come along," he whispered.

"Think you'll ever find her?"

He leaned close, the scent of leather and spice that always surrounded him moving like a wind storm through April's senses. "Oh, I found the right woman a long time ago. But I'm still waiting for her to come around to my terms."

April's heart banged hard against her ribs. Her hands trembled so much, she had to hold onto one of the mugs in front of her. "What…what are your terms, Reed?"

His voice whispered with a rawhide scrape against her ear. "I only have one stipulation, actually. I want that woman to love me with all her heart. I want her to love me, only me, enough to stay by my side for a lifetime and beyond."

April looked up at him then and saw the love there in his stalking-cat eyes—the love and the challenge. "You don't ask for much, do you, cowboy?"

"Doesn't seem like much if you look at it the right way."

Then he turned and sauntered back to the table where his parents waited in questioning wide-eyed silence.

And April was left to look at the scene with a whole new perspective. And a whole new set of fears.

Chapter Seven

April came into the kitchen the next morning only to find Flora slumped in a chair, crying.

"What's wrong?" April said, rushing to the woman's side. "Is it—is it my father?"

She'd sat with him late into the night, pouring her heart out to him, telling him that she still loved Reed, only now she didn't think she deserved to be loved back. Telling him all about her fears and her reservations, her hopes and her dreams. She'd checked on him just minutes ago and Lynette had assured her he was sleeping.

"No, no, *querida*," Flora said, reaching up a hand to April. "It's not your papa. It's…" She waved the other hand in the air. "It's Tomás. That boy is giving us so much trouble lately."

April breathed a sigh of relief only to see the concern in Flora's rich brown eyes. "What's Tomás doing that's so bad it would make you cry?"

Flora shook her head. "He shows no respect. His parents—they both work all day long—they let him run wild. No restraint. And that Adan—*élse malo*—he's mean, very mean. He's going to get in big, big trouble, that one." She lapsed into a string of Spanish, then went back to wringing her hands.

From what April could glean from Flora's rantings, she gathered Tomás and Adan had taken Horaz's pickup for a joyride and had been stopped by the sheriff for speeding. There was a hefty ticket to pay. And Horaz would probably have to be the one to pay it, since Tomás's parents were heavily in debt from overextending themselves.

"I'm sorry, Flora," April said, patting the distraught woman on the shoulder. "Do you want *me* to pay the fine?"

"No," Flora said, getting up to wipe her eyes on her gathered apron. "That wouldn't help. The boy needs to learn how to fix his own problems. He will work it off. His grandfather will see to that, even if my son thinks Tomás can do no wrong. No wrong for big football star."

April knew enough to understand the implications of that. High-school football was a very popular sport all over Texas. And Tomás was a gifted athlete, she deduced from everything she'd heard since coming home, which meant his other, less noble traits would sometimes be overlooked for the sake of winning the game. Unless he pushed things too far. "If Tomás rebels against authority too much, he might get kicked off the football team next season."

"*Sí, sí,*" Flora replied. "This is what I try to tell my son. This is what Horaz tries to explain to Tomás. Heads of wood, those two. Heads—stubborn heads. *Loco.*"

April smiled at Flora's sputtering condemnations in spite of the seriousness of the situation. "I could try to talk to Tomás," she offered.

Flora grabbed April's hand. "You have too much—too much to worry with. Tomás, he is my responsibility. Mine and his grandfather's, since we've been put in charge of him for the summer. His own parents are too busy to see the problems." Another harsh string of Spanish followed.

"I love Tomás, too, remember?" April replied, remembering how she used to take the young Tomás horseback-riding when she was a teenager. "What if I get Reed to talk to him? He looks up to Reed, or at least he used to when he was little."

Flora's eyes lit up. "*Sí,* Reed. Everyone looks up to Reed. And Tomás has heard the stories of Reed Garrison. Now there was a football star, that one. He never gave his parents any trouble. And he was the best in his day."

"Yes, he was," April replied, her memories of crisp autumn nights so real she thought she could smell the smoke from the bonfires, hear the words of the high-school song. And she could clearly see Reed's smiling, loving face from the crowd of padded players on a green field. He'd always searched for her in the cheerleading line, giving her a wave for promise and hope.

What had happened to that promise and hope?

"Will you ask him?"

Flora's plea brought April back into the here and now, all the memories gone in the blink of an eye.

"Of course," April said, wanting to reassure Flora. But just thinking of having to face Reed again after he had thrown down the gauntlet last night made her want to run and hide away in her room.

But April was done with running and

hiding. Her father wasn't going to get out of that deathbed. Reed wasn't going to back down. She had to stand up and take responsibility for her actions and her mistakes. It was up to her now to make sure the Big M kept on going. And if that meant she'd have to counsel one of their own—she and Reed together—then so be it.

At least dealing with Tomás would take her mind off her father and her feelings for Reed.

"I'll call Reed right now," she told Flora. "Just let me have a cup of coffee first."

Flora hopped up, her hands fluttering in embarrassment. "I'm so sorry. I should have—"

"Don't be silly," April said, waving the woman back down. "I'll get both of us a cup of coffee. And maybe some of that wonderful cinnamon coffee cake you always have stashed around here."

Flora smiled at that. "Better with melted butter on it. You can slip it into the microwave. Or I can do that."

"You sit," April commanded. "I'll take care of breakfast."

She wasn't sure if she could actually eat, but if Flora's cooking didn't entice her, nothing would.

She thought about Reed again. She'd thought about Reed for most of the night. She wondered if her father had heard her talking about him last night, had understood how strong her feelings were. How scared she was to make that final step toward Reed, that step that meant family and home, total commitment, total surrender.

She had a feeling Reed wouldn't want it any other way, and why should she blame him for that? She longed for that kind of love herself, even if she was terrified to try it.

On the other hand, what about her job at Satire? She had responsibilities there, too. And she loved what she did there, the things she'd accomplished. She was good at her job. How could she walk away from something that she enjoyed, a career that gave her contentment and a measure of accomplishment? A career, she reminded herself, that oftentimes took control over her entire life, leaving her alone at the end of the day. When she looked back, if she hadn't had Summer and Autumn there with her in New York, she probably would have been lonely and miserable, in spite of the friends she'd made at work.

No, April told herself with a fierce denial, coming home has just brought too many things to the surface. I can't just abandon my career. I can't do that.

Bringing the coffee and food to the table where Flora sat, April put her own turmoil to rest for now and managed to smile over at the other woman. "I guess being a grandparent is just as hard as being a parent."

Flora nodded, took the coffee with a *"Gracias."* "You think once you raise them, everything will be okay. It's never okay. You worry." She pressed a hand to her heart. "You worry here, you hold them close, here, always."

"I guess my father worried about me,

even when he knew I was doing all right
in New York."

"*Sí*. He always talked about you. Very
proud, that one. Always longed to see you.
Especially when—"

She stopped short.

"Especially when he was drinking?"
April asked, finishing Flora's unspoken
thoughts.

Flora nodded, tears brimming her eyes
again. "A good man, a very good man. But
the drink—it made him say things he
couldn't take back. Very sad."

April felt that sadness down to her very
bones. So much time wasted, so much love
lost. She didn't think she wanted that kind
of love, the kind that made a powerful, vir-
ile man turn into a wasted-away skeleton
of himself.

Did she love Reed too much? Could she
ever accept that love, with all the stipula-
tions it required?

Then she remembered Reed's words to
her last night. I only have one stipula-

tion.... *Doesn't seem like much if you look at it the right way.*

I don't know the right way, Reed, she thought. I don't know how to look at love without seeing the pain involved.

She glanced over at Flora and found the woman's eyes closed and her lips moving. "Flora?"

"I pray," Flora said, her eyes still closed. "I pray for you and Mr. Stuart, and Reed and my Horaz. And especially for my Tomás." Then she opened her eyes and smiled. "God has already answered part of that prayer. You and Reed, you will see to my grandson, *sí?*"

"*Sí,*" April replied, lifting her eyes to the heavens.

"*I hear you, Lord,*" she said out loud.

Flora smiled and took a long sip of her coffee.

April wanted to see him.

Reed let that bit of information settle into a simmering stew inside his gut. It hurt to think about her. The physical pain of loving her was getting to him. It had been okay when she was off far away, across the country. Time, bitterness and distance had faded his pain, and the soft rage he'd felt at her leaving, into a kind of mellowed photo album of memories. Memories he'd hidden away until now.

And he hadn't helped matters by challenging her last night. He'd practically asked her to stay, right there in the kitchen, with his well-meaning parents watching in rapt awe. He'd almost blown it. Again.

"I'm needing some guidance here, Lord," he said aloud as he pulled his rumbling pickup into the sprawling side yard of the big house. *"I've got a nice, easy thing going here. I have my bit of land now, a place to call my own. I've worked hard these last few years. You have blessed my life, Lord. Only one thing was missing."*

And that one thing was now waiting for him out by the crystal-blue waters of the swimming pool. Ending his prayers on a silent plea for strength and restraint, Reed opened the wrought-iron gate leading to the back of the property. He found April waiting for him right where she said she'd be. For once.

She was wearing a golden-beige sleeveless pantsuit of some sort. Linen, his mother might say. Soft linen that flowed around her like a summer wind. Her jewelry reflected the same gold of her clothes, simmering and rich against her porcelain skin.

Reed had to stop and take in a breath. She looked like some noble ancient princess, sitting there on the chaise. Until he looked into her dark eyes.

"What's wrong?"

April gestured to the cushioned chair beside the umbrella table. "We need to talk."

Oh, boy. He didn't like that look in her eyes. The last time she'd told him they needed to talk, she'd already packed her bags for New York and just wanted to tell him goodbye.

He sank down in defeat, took off his hat and said, "So, talk."

"It's about Tomás," she said, letting out a breath with each word.

"Tomás?" Confused but relieved, Reed leaned forward. "What's up with Tomás?"

She handed him a glass of lemonade, then settled back on the chaise. "Flora is very upset with him." She told him the whole story then. "She wanted me to ask you to try to reason with him, tell him to take it easy and be careful. You know, a kind of man-to-man talk."

"Why me?" Reed asked. "And why do you look so sad and serious?"

She shrugged, causing her chunky jewelry to settle back around her neck. Reed eyed the pretty stones and glowing gold. "Everyone around here looks up to you, Reed. Flora thought you'd be the natural choice for the job. And if I look sad, well, I am. But that's not something for you to worry about. Flora needs your help right now."

He got up and paced around the rock-encrusted pool deck. "That's me. Good ol' Reed. Salt of the earth. The go-to man." For everyone except her, of course. Shrugging, he started to leave. "I'll talk to Tomás. He's supposed to be helping me with some fence work today anyway. Give us a chance to have a nice long chat."

"Are you angry at me?"

She was right behind him, so close he caught the whiff of her floral perfume. "No," he said with a long sigh. "I'm not angry at anyone. Just tired and confused, is all. And sad, just like you." He turned to face her, looked down at her dark curling hair, her big brown eyes, and her beautiful mouth, and felt the flare of that old flame, burning strong inside his heart.

Then he did something he would later call very stupid. He kissed her, right there in the broad open daylight, by the swimming pool, with the many windows of the long, rambling house open for all inside to see. It was a stupid move because he'd steeled himself to go slow, to take things easy. He didn't want to spook her.

She didn't seem spooked in his arms.

She kind of melted against him, her hands touching his hair as a soft sigh drifted between them. Her sigh. Or maybe it was his. Reed couldn't be sure. But he was very sure of one thing. And that one thing made his hard heart turn to mush.

April still loved him, too. This he knew with the instinct of a man who always knew what he wanted, even when he wasn't sure how to go about getting it. He aimed to find the right way to go about winning April back. For good.

With that declaration pumping through his head, he let her go and stared down at her, hoping he didn't seem too triumphant. "That…that wasn't supposed to happen," he said with a ragged breath. "I mean, we were discussing this situation with Tomás, right?"

She managed to nod. "Right. I'm not sure how—"

"I know how," he interrupted, one finger tracing a wayward curl of rich brown hair that had managed to find its way across her cheek. "One look, April. That's all it takes. One look and I remember everything. And I want to hold you, and protect you and kiss you."

He saw the fear rising up in her eyes like a mist coming in over the river. "We shouldn't—"

"I know. It's the wrong time. It's not fair to either of us. But there it is. We kissed each other, and, unless I'm mistaken, you enjoyed it just as much as I did."

She lowered her head, staring at the gently moving water in the serene pool. "Reed, we need to concentrate on my father right now. And all the problems on this ranch. The vandalism, and now this with Tomás." Then she looked back up at him. "But I've learned something, coming home. This place doesn't just run itself. A million little problems crop up each day. And I want to thank you for always…for helping my father through all of this. I know it hasn't been easy for you. You could have left—"

"I wanted to stay," he said, the old anger coming back to numb the joy he'd felt at having her back in his arms. "I will stay. No matter what happens. *This* is my home. This will always be *my* home. Is that clear, April?"

His own anger was reflected back at him through the haze of anger in her eyes. "Very clear, Reed." Then she turned to head back inside the house. "Just talk to Tomás. Flora and Horaz don't need to be worrying about him right now."

"Yes, ma'am." He tipped his hat and headed back to the gate.

So much for thinking she still loved him. She did, he knew that. But she wouldn't admit that to him, or to herself, either. She'd watch her father die, bury him, then she'd go right back to New York. Running scared again.

And she'd leave Reed here waiting, all over again.

Chapter Eight

You've got mail.

Summer called out to her cousin. "Hey, April's sent us an update. Want me to read it out loud?"

"Sure," Autumn said, distracted by the mound of paperwork in front of her. Tax time. It was a killer, but it paid the rent. And being a CPA for one of the largest accounting firms in New York meant she was right in the thick of things. Just the way she liked it. She liked numbers and charts. She liked proof. Everything had to add up, make sense. Only two more days of this intense tax season frenzy, and then she could relax a bit. Not that she ever actually relaxed.

"Go ahead, I'm listening," she called to Summer.

"Okay."

"'Daddy is about the same. Uncle Richard called Reed the other day, then called me. He hopes to come and visit this weekend. He said I should ask y'all to come home, but Autumn's surely busy right now. Maybe in a few weeks, if Daddy can last that long. If not, well, I guess y'all will have to come when things change, when he's gone. He looks so frail, so old. How did I let things get this bad?'"

Summer stopped reading. "No mention of *my* daddy, huh? No mention of Uncle James and Aunt Elsie. Of course, they're probably off on the yacht, unaware of anyone else but themselves."

"Your bitterness is showing," Autumn called.

"You think?"

"Just read me the rest, so I can get back to work."

Summer turned back to the computer.

"'Reed kissed me this morning.'"

That brought Autumn careening across the big lofty living room so fast, the magnolia-scented candles Summer always kept lit flickered from the stirring of air. "What?"

"Says so right here," Summer replied, pointing at the words on the screen. "Reed kissed April."

"Oh, my." Autumn sank down on a cushioned polka-dot footstool near Summer's chair. "What else does she say?"

"'We were by the swimming pool. It was mid-morning. He kissed me right there in the sunshine. And it felt as if we'd never been apart. I don't think this is smart right now, even if it felt so right. I have to think about Daddy. And did I tell y'all that Daddy thinks I'm home for good, that he expects me to stay here and run the Big M?'"

"Makes sense," Autumn murmured.

"She will inherit it after he's gone. I mean, Daddy and Uncle James will get their parts, but they both gave up running the Big M long ago. And Uncle Stuart is the oldest. She's his daughter. Makes sense to me that he'd leave the majority of the ranch holdings to his only heir."

"Shouldn't we be jealous or something?" Summer asked.

Autumn slapped her on the arm. "Of what? Our parents have just as much loot as Uncle Stuart. And we're not hurting, either."

"I was just teasing," Summer said, sticking out her tongue. "I don't want any of it, anyway. Besides, my parents are too busy spending their part to worry about actually thinking about *my* future."

Autumn scowled at her cousin. "You need therapy."

"I don't need some overpaid shrink to tell me that my parents don't care about me," Summer retorted. "Now, can we get back to worrying about April?"

"Sure," Autumn replied, more worried about Summer. She had a chip on her shoulder that seriously needed shaking. But Autumn wouldn't be the one to do it. "Go on," she said, nudging Summer. "Keep reading."

"'I don't know what to do. I planned to return to New York and Satire. I've built up a career there and I have a good chance of getting a promotion when we break into ready-to-wear this fall.'"

"Head of ready-to-wear marketing," Summer said, nodding. "She'd be so good at getting Satire's ready-to-wear off the ground. Trendy new threads and up-scale department stores—stock should go right through the roof. Glad I invested early."

"It would mean lots of traveling to all the various stores," Autumn said. "All over the country and around the world. And I'm the one who told you to invest early, so you're welcome. We both should make some money off this one."

"How can she run the ranch and do that, too?" Summer shot back, ignoring her cousin's other remarks.

"What does she say?"

"'I don't think I can do both—run this place and keep my job, let alone get a promotion.'"

Summer jabbed the computer. "Told you."

"Just keep reading," Autumn said, scanning the words on the screen. "I've got to get back to work."

Summer turned and started reading again.

"'I'm in such a fix. But all of that aside, I have to be near Daddy right now. I talk to him every night, tell him all the things I wished I'd said before. I'm not sure he can hear me, but it feels so good to pour my heart out to him. Why did I wait so long? Why did I let myself fall back in love with Reed? I've realized that all this time, he's been waiting for me to come back, and now that I'm here, it's for all the wrong reasons. I'm home to watch my father die. So Reed is being kind and patient and undemanding, but I've also realized that maybe, just maybe, I've been waiting for Reed all these years, too. I guess I always thought he'd come for me, you know? That somehow, he'd come to New York and tell me he wanted me back home, with him. Isn't that silly?'"

"She's completely stressed," Summer said, finishing the e-mail. "Maybe I should go there, be with her. She's getting too caught up in memories of her first love. That's dangerous. She shouldn't get her hopes up."

Autumn stared at her cousin. "What's wrong with a little hope? Uncle Stu is dying. And she still loves Reed. What's wrong with hoping that they might actually get to be together?"

Summer jumped up, headed for the kitchen. "I just wouldn't pin too much hope on a happily-ever-after," she called over her shoulder. "She's been through enough."

Then she came back to the sofa with a

container of yogurt. "Maybe I should just go there and help her get her head straight."

"You could go to *lend her your support,*" Autumn said, "not shatter her illusions. You have gobs of vacation time accumulated." She started back toward her desk. "Then as soon as tax season is over, I could come, too. If—"

"If it's not too late," Summer finished. "I'll see what I can arrange at work. Take a few days. I could use a vacation anyway."

"That's an understatement," Autumn replied. "But if you go and your parents do show up, don't make a scene, all right? It's not the time to make a big deal out of past hurts, Summer."

"Yes, ma'am," Summer said, saluting her cousin, her frown pulling her oval face down. "You're so calm and collected, Autumn. How do you do that?"

"Do what?"

"Always stay in control. I mean, I blow up, shout, fight, pout. But not you. Always got it together."

"You make that sound like a sin."

"It is, if you can't ever let go and just—react."

"I don't recall reading about that in the Bible."

"I do," Summer countered. "Something in Psalms, about asking the Lord to cleanse us from our secret faults."

"I don't need cleansing and I don't harbor any secret thoughts. I'm just fine."

"Well, I guess I do—harbor secret thoughts, that is," Summer replied, her eyes downcast. "I guess I got me a lot of cleansing to do. I cry out, just as King David did, but sometimes I don't think the Lord is listening."

Autumn touched her cousin's arm. "Well, just don't do it when you get to the Big M. I mean, don't cry out at your parents or raise a ruckus. Ask God to ease your famous temper. April needs us to be strong and supportive."

"If I go, I won't make a scene, I promise," Summer replied.

Autumn hoped her volatile cousin meant that. It would be bad if Summer lost her cool while Uncle Stu lay dying.

"You know Mr. Stuart is dying, right?" Reed asked Tomás as they rode the fences the next morning.

Tomás held on to the dash of the hefty red pickup with one hand while he worked on adjusting the radio dial to a hard-rock station. "Yeah."

Reed pushed the boy's hand away and turned the radio off. "And you understand that we all need to rally around the family right now, not cause any hassles?"

Tomás glanced over at him, his dark eyes slashing an attitude a mile wide underneath the fringe of his silky black bangs. "You mean, like I shouldn't get speeding tickets and cause an uproar with my grandparents?"

"Yeah, I mean that," Reed said with a sigh. "Want to talk about it?"

"I wasn't going that fast."

"You just got your license. You might need to take it easy until you're a little more experienced."

"I *am* experienced, Reed. I've been driving all over this ranch since I was twelve."

Reed nodded. "I did the same thing. Best place to learn to drive. But driving on these dirt lanes is a whole lot different from driving out on the highway or up on the Interstate. I'd hate for something to happen to you or your buddies. And I don't think Adan's parents would approve of this kind of behavior, either."

"We're okay, Adan and me. Or we would be if everybody would just leave us alone."

Reed stopped the truck near a sagging barbed-wire fence, then got out. "It's our job to hassle you, man. Keep you in shape. We wouldn't want the star of the football team to get in trouble."

"I'm covered there," Tomás said with a twist of a grin as he slammed the truck door. "Coach understands me."

"I'm sure he does," Reed said, wondering when things had changed so much in high-school sports. His coach had kept a tight rein on all the players—curfew, good grades, no late-night shenanigans, no drugs or liquor. A long list of no-nos. Nowadays, it seemed as long as a boy could throw a ball or run fast, he could get away with indiscretions of all kinds. "Listen," he said as he and Tomás rounded the truck, "we all care about you. If we didn't care, we'd just let you run loose."

"My parents let me do whatever I want," Tomás retorted. "*They* trust me."

Reed stared over at the young boy. Tomás was handsome in a dark, brooding way. A way that could lead to trouble down the road. And from the pained expression on the boy's face, Reed decided Tomás wished his parents did care a little bit more. A whole lot more.

"Do your parents know about the ticket?"

"Yeah, sure. No big deal."

"Uh-huh." Reed could only guess what his own father would have done in the same situation. It would have been a *very* big deal. "Well, your grandparents think differently. So…Horaz is giving you yard duty on top of your other chores."

"What?" Tomás threw down the coil of wire he had gathered from the back of the truck. "I have to mow that big yard? That is so *not* fair."

Reed shrugged. "Life is so not fair at times. But you have to roll with the punches. You got the speeding ticket. Now you get to do the time."

"But Grandpa said he'd help me pay it."

"Yes, and because he's doing that, he expects you to work off some of the price."

"That's just not right."

"Neither is going sixty-five in a thirty-five-mile-per-hour zone. Can't have it both ways, Tomás."

"My dad says I can have it all, if I just keep playing football. He says one day, I can own a ranch like the Big M."

"Your dad is proud of you, I reckon," Reed replied, shaking his head. "But first, get a good education, and stay out of trouble. I sincerely hope you become a success in football, Tomás. College and pro. But don't count on that. Have a backup plan."

"Did you?" Tomás asked, his expression clearly stating the obvious. Reed had had the same dream and it ended when he messed up his knee.

The boy's pointed question should have hurt, but Reed knew in his heart he was content with his lot in life. He could deal with it. Well, almost. "As a matter of fact, I did have a backup plan," he told Tomás. "I always wanted to have my own spot of land, right here near the Big M. And now I do."

"Yeah, and look how long you had to work to get that," Tomás remarked, his tone smug and sure.

Reed grabbed Tomás by one of his thick leather gloves. "Hey, I'm proud of my land. I worked hard to get it. I wouldn't have it any other way. And you'd better learn right now, son, there aren't any short-cuts in life."

"You sound like my *abuelo*. But then, both of you have spent most of your lives catering to the whim of the big man, right?"

Reed wanted to smack the kid, but he held his temper in check. "We weren't catering to anyone's whims, Tomás. We were making a living—an honest living. Your grandparents have had a good life here on the Big M. Stuart Maxwell has made sure of that. And he's always helped my family, too. Don't bite the hand that feeds you, and don't ever disrespect Stuart Maxwell again."

Tomás looked down, his sheepish expression making him look young and unsure. "I just want a better life, Reed. I just want more."

"We all want that, kid. But…just make sure you go about getting the good in life in the right way. Remember your roots, your faith in God. Remember where you come from. Don't do anything stupid, okay?"

Tomás looked doubtful, then shrugged. "Yeah, sure. I'll be careful."

"I hope so," Reed said. He'd have to pray that Tomás had listened to him. Really listened.

April tried to listen to what the preacher was saying in church the next Sunday. But her mind wandered off in several different directions, maybe because Reed and his parents were sitting right behind her. She could almost feel his catlike eyes on her.

He'd been standoffish and quiet since their kiss. He'd been avoiding her. He came by and called to check on her daddy and give her updates on the ranch. That was something at least, since he could send any one of the many hands they had on the Big M to do that job.

But then, Reed had always been a meticulous details man. He'd always been thorough in anything he did—from playing football to starting a vegetable garden to dating the rich girl from the big house.

In fact, she had to remind herself, he'd been so complete in his love for her, in what he hoped their future would be like, that he'd spelled it out in detail for her over and over again.

And she'd let him believe she wanted the same things.

She looked up at Reverend Hughes. What had he just said? His mercy endures forever? Did God show mercy to those who turned from him? Would God show mercy to her dear, dying father? Would God show her that same mercy?

I was scared, Lord. I was so scared.

She could understand now. Her heart and her head had matured a hundred times over. If she had married Reed back then, she would have made his life—the simple life he'd always wanted—miserable.

Because I was miserable.

Why couldn't she just be happy? Why had she gone so far away to find her own brand of happiness?

Because I was scared. I'd lost my mother.

I'd watched my father deteriorate into a mire of grief. Even going away to college hadn't helped. The weekends at home only brought the pain back into a sharply focused kaleidoscope of anger and grief.

That grief had been so overwhelming, so thick with despair, April had felt as if she were drowning. And she felt that same pulling feeling now, which was why she'd taken a precious hour away from her father to come to church.

I had to get away, to find some peace, some space.

Back then, and now, for just a little while.

But she didn't want to repeat the same mistakes, follow the same path again. *Not this time, Lord.*

All those years ago, she'd hurt Reed. And she'd never wanted to hurt Reed. She loved him. Loved him still.

I need Your mercy, Lord.

April thought about her father. Asked God to show all of them his tender mercies. She had to take it one day at a time. That was all she could do at this point. She couldn't think beyond her father and what lay ahead— Even if she did feel Reed's eyes on her, willing her to think of him and their future.

When April got home an hour later, Flora greeted her in the kitchen. "I just got here myself. Lunch is in the oven, *querida*. Oh, and you have a message from a Katherine Price. Phone was ringing when I came in. Lynette can't hear it back there. We've got that phone turned off, so we don't disturb your father."

"Katherine called?" April took the note Flora had scribbled. "Urgent."

"*Sí*," Flora said, taking off her church hat so she could serve up the pot roast she'd left in the oven on warm. "Is she someone from your work?"

"My supervisor, the CEO of public relations," April said, reaching for the phone. "She's probably wondering why I haven't called in to work."

"You have enough to worry about."

"Yes, but I also have responsibilities back in New York. Although I pretty much cleared my desk before I left."

"You should eat first," Flora said, concern marring her tranquil eyes.

"I will later. You and Horaz go ahead. Are any of your family joining you for Sunday dinner today?"

"No," Flora said with a sigh as she tied her apron. "My son, Dakota—you remember him—he took his wife on a weekend to Dallas. Left us in charge of Tomás, of course."

Her fingers on the phone, April asked, "Did Reed talk to Tomás?"

"*Sí*, but the boy was very angry still. Blamed us for his troubles. He's not happy to be doing yard work."

April had to smile at that. "It's going to get hot out very soon. But then, Tomás should be used to sweating, what with football practice all the time."

Flora nodded. "He's just not used to authority. *Obstinado*, that one."

April shook her head. "I hope things get better. Now, you get your lunch ready while I make this call."

She left Flora humming a gospel tune. Heading out onto the long tiled verandah by the swimming pool, April dialed Katherine Price's home number.

What did her boss want on a Sunday afternoon?

Her stomach twisting in knots, April waited for the phone to ring. Just one more thing to deal with. She didn't need problems at work while she had so much going on here at the Big M.

But then, she'd already decided she couldn't handle both.

She once again prayed for that mercy Reverend Hughes had talked about. Mercy, and strength. She needed both for the long days ahead.

Chapter Nine

"April, darling, how in the world are you?"

Hearing the lilt in Katherine's voice made April breathe a sigh of relief. If her boss was in a bad mood, she wouldn't have called April "darling."

"I'm okay, all things considered," April replied into the phone. "I got your message. Is everything all right?"

"First, how's your father?"

April could envision the sophisticated leader of Satire public relations and marketing worldwide sitting on a chaise lounge on the sprawling balcony of her Park Avenue apartment, sipping an espresso and eating biscotti. But she was touched that Katherine had thought of her father before rushing headlong into business.

"My father is about the same, Katherine. The doctor comes by each day and tells us there is nothing else to be done. He hasn't opened his eyes for days now."

"You poor dear," Katherine said. "I wish there was something *I* could do."

April couldn't take any sympathy. She'd fall apart and she didn't want to do that in front of fashionable, together Katherine Price. "You can tell me what's happening at Satire. Why you called with an urgent message."

"Oh, right. Well, darling, you know we're in the midst of getting prepared to launch the ready-to-wear this fall. And of course, you've done such a great job with the preliminary marketing. You left things in good shape and the marketing and public relations departments are following your guidelines to the letter."

"But?" April asked, hearing the worry in Katherine's voice. "Is there something else that needs to be done?"

"Well, darling, you know I wouldn't ask if it weren't really important."

"Just tell me," April said, dread making her words sound sharp.

"Darling, is there any way you can fly back to New York for a couple of days? It's just a glitch or two with one of the department stores. They're trying to renege on the original contract. They want to cut back on their advance orders for the fall line."

"The contracts are ironclad," April replied, thinking there was no way she could leave her father right now. It was ironic how her whole perspective on work had changed.

"We know that, April," Katherine said through a long-suffering sigh. "But the store in question is giving us grief. Frankly, I think they're about to declare bankruptcy and they're trying to clean house, so to speak, before this goes public. That's why we need you here to negotiate—through our lawyers, of course. You always know what kind of spin to put on this type of crisis."

A crisis. Katherine Price, the head of PR for one of the most successful fashion houses in the world, thought that one department store trying to go south was a crisis.

April wanted to tell her that she now knew what a real crisis was like, but it wasn't Katherine's fault that her father was so ill. "Which store is it?" she asked, wondering how she was going to take care of this without going back to New York.

"It's Fairchild's," Katherine replied. "You know they've already had to restructure and lay off employees nationwide. They were banking on Satire to help them get back in the thick of things—they haven't had a winning label in their stores for a very long time now, just mediocre stuff all around—but it looks as if someone within their ranks got cold feet about overextending the stores with this massive order."

"Would that someone be Danny Pierson, by any chance?" April asked, the pieces of the puzzle beginning to come together in her mind.

"Why, as a matter of fact, he's the one who called me personally," Katherine said, surprise echoing out over the phone line. "Is there something about him I should be aware of?"

"Only that I dated him last year and it ended rather badly," April replied. "He didn't take the breakup very well."

"Oh, my. How long did you two date?"

"About six months," April said, remembering what a pompous control freak Danny had been. "He…made certain demands I couldn't meet."

"And now he's making those same demands on Satire," Katherine said. "Darling, you know not to mix business with pleasure. How could you let this happen?"

April held a finger to her forehead and pushed at the bangs covering her eyes. "I didn't let anything happen, Katherine. He didn't work for Fairchild's when we were an item. He went with them right after the beginning of the year, this year. And I'm sure he's just now discovered our contract with them. I can't imagine he'd be doing this to get back at me, though. He could jeopardize not only Fairchild's reputation, but his own."

"Then you agree you should come back and handle this?" Katherine asked, her tone firm.

"I didn't say that," April replied. "I think all we have to do is tell our lawyers to meet with Fairchild's and explain how things stand. That should get Danny to back off."

"And what if he doesn't? Darling, you know how important this ready-to-wear launch is. We've been working on this for eighteen months straight."

"I realize that," April said, "but, Katherine, I can't leave my father right now. He's…he's not going to last much longer."

Silence. Then a long sigh. "I understand. And you have my utmost sympathy, dear.

But we need someone who can sweet-talk the powers at Fairchild's. And that would be you."

"What if I call Danny?" April asked. "Maybe I can nip this in the bud before it goes any further."

"You'd be willing to do that?"

"I can try. It's a start, at least. And I'll call all my contacts at Fairchild's and find out if this is something Danny just cooked up, or if it's really serious."

"Well, I guess if that's the best we can do right now—"

"I'll take care of it," April said, her insides recoiling at the idea of having to deal with slimy Danny Pierson again. But then, it was part of her job to negotiate tricky situations with clients. And there was a lot riding on this deal, as Katherine had reminded her. "I have Danny's number in my business files. I'll call him first thing tomorrow."

"Thank you so much," Katherine replied. "And keep me posted on this."

"I will, of course," April said. "I'll get this cleared up. Don't worry."

"I know you will. And darling, I really am so sorry about your father."

"Thank you," April said.

When she hung up the phone, she turned to find Reed standing in the doorway.

He looked sheepish. "Sorry, I didn't mean to listen in. Flora told me you were here in the den."

"It's okay," April said, raising a hand in the air. "Just a problem at work."

"You don't need a problem at work. You have enough to worry about right here."

"I know, I know. And I don't need everyone reminding me of that, either."

He stalked into the room. "Sorry. Is everything all right at work?"

"Just a little mixup with one of our clients. I'll get it straightened out."

"Do you need a break from all of this?"

"No," she said. "I'm afraid to leave the house. He's so frail and quiet." Right now, she really wanted to just run away from everything and everyone. Especially Reed. He was hovering and that made her nervous. "Did you need to talk to me?"

"No. Just wanted to check in. See how you're holding up."

"How do I look?" she asked, the words snapping out like a whip against hide.

"Like you need a break, just as I said."

He moved toward her, but she backed away. "I don't need a break. I'm fine. I just need to think about how to take care of this problem without having to go back to New York."

The silence between them told her he was weighing her words. Weighing and judging, she imagined.

"So you want me to go?" he finally asked.

"That's entirely up to you, Reed." She looked up at him, the hurt in his eyes making her wince at her harsh attitude. If she could be honest with him, she'd rush into his arms and beg him never to leave. But she wasn't ready to take that step. "I just need some time alone," she said.

"Okay. Mom wanted me to invite you over to supper tonight."

"I can't leave the house, Reed. You know how things are."

This time, he watched her back away again, then moved after her until he had her in his arms. "Hey, I do know how things are. We can have supper here again. Or we can just send something over, if you don't want company."

"I can't eat," she said, hot tears brimming in her eyes. "I can't think beyond his next breath."

"I know," he said, kissing the top of her hair. "I wish there was something I could do."

His gentleness almost did her in, but she took a calming breath and let out a shaky laugh. "Funny, that's what my boss just said, right after she practically ordered me back to New York."

Reed lifted her chin with a finger. "You're not going back right now, are you?"

Offended at his possessive tone, she

pulled away. "No, of course not. But I'm going to have to make some calls, fight some fires. I still have a job—or at least I did when I left New York."

She could feel the condemnation again, see it in his eyes as he spoke. "Yeah, I guess you can't just forget about your work."

"No, I can't. But I'm not leaving my father." At his raised eyebrows, she added, "Does that surprise you, Reed? If so, then I guess you don't know me as well as you think you do."

He stepped back. "I thought I knew you, but the old April would probably have taken off by now. This April, the woman I'm looking at right now… I think she has staying power."

"Impressed?"

"No, proud," he said before turning to leave. Then he whirled at the arched doorway. "I am proud of you, April. You're doing the right thing."

Before she could think of a mean, smart retort, he left the room, the sound of his cowboy boots clicking with precision against the tiled floor.

"I don't know the right thing to do," April said, her plea lifting up to the heavens. "I don't know what I should do or say."

She silently prayed that God would give her the grace to do what she had to do. And that Reed would continue to be proud of her, no matter what decisions she had to make over the next few weeks.

He wasn't very proud of himself, Reed decided later that night. He was trying. Heaven help him, he wanted to do and say the right things when it came to April.

But the woman just brought out the worst in him.

As well as the best.

So the subject of New York City was definitely a sore spot between them. But then, Reed couldn't understand why anyone would want to leave a place like the Big M. The rolling pastures and hills, the trees and ponds, the rows and rows of crape myrtle growing all over Paris, the Red River nearby, all the work a big ranch required—all of this was his lifeblood. His family had lived and worked on this ranch for generations. He was as rooted here as the cottonwoods and the *bois d'arc,* or bow dark trees, as the locals called them.

He just couldn't understand why April didn't feel the same toward her home. What had driven her away from the place she'd always seemed to love.

Grief.

The one word echoed around him like a dove's soft coo. He remembered April telling him that her father's grief had stifled and scared her. But what about her own grief? Maybe she hadn't actually worked through her own pain after her mother's death.

No, instead she'd run from it. And she was still running. But she was being brave in coming back to her home, no matter the horrible memories and the sadness that seemed to shroud the big house these days. Maybe she was home in the flesh, but her spirit was somewhere far away. Her spirit was lost in maybes and what ifs and what-might-have-beens. Just as his own seemed to be, Reed decided.

When he coupled her immense grief back then with the fact that he had been constantly hovering with unsolicited advice and unwelcome demands, asking her about marriage and family, well, no wonder the woman had escaped. He shouldn't have pushed her so hard. But he'd wanted a future with her so very much. He still did. But she was grieving yet again.

The phone rang, jarring him out of the troubled thoughts that were pounding at his brain.

"Hello," he said, his tone full of irritation.

"Son, are you all right?" his mother asked.

"Just dandy. What's up?"

"I wondered why you didn't come by for dinner. You and April."

His mother's words were full of questions and implications.

"April wasn't in the mood for company,

Mom. And I don't think she's been eating very much at all, either. I think she's lost even more weight."

"That girl eats like a bird. Always did."

"Well, I guess her appetite is taking a hit these days."

"Did you offer to stay there at the house with her?"

Reed lifted his gaze to the heavens for support. "Mom, she didn't want me there."

"Oh, I think you're wrong there," his confident mother responded. "I think she wants you there, but she's afraid to voice that."

"Well, I can't second-guess her. Never could."

"The Lord has a plan for you two. I've always believed that."

"Well, then let's just let the Lord show us the way," Reed said, his tone lighter this time. He knew his mother meant well, and he loved her for caring. But he also knew that if he and April were ever to have a life together, then it would have to be something they both wanted, regardless of how strongly his mother felt about it.

It would be up to God to intervene.

Reed thanked his mother for calling, then hung up the phone. He was just about to go to bed when Shep started barking and pawing at the back door. "Need a walk, old fellow?" Reed asked as he swung the door open.

He stepped outside and heard the noise at about the same time Shep took off toward the small storage shed behind the house.

Someone was out there.

Shep barked with renewed frenzy as he galloped toward the shed. Reed hurried after the dog.

"Who's there?" Reed called, hoping it was just an armadillo or a possum.

When he heard footsteps echoing out behind the building, he knew the intruder was human. He ran toward the shed, listening as Shep's angry, agitated bark filled the quiet night.

Reed reached the shed just as a shadowy

figure cleared the wooden fence behind the shed. "Hey, you," Reed called, "too chicken to show your face?"

All he heard was the sound of hurried footsteps and then the roar of what sounded like a four-wheeler taking off. And Shep, barking at the fence.

When he was sure that the intruders were gone, Reed called to his dog. "Let's go get a flashlight, boy."

Reed got a high-beam light out of his truck, then inched his way around the out-buildings. He saw footprints near the back of the shed, but couldn't find anything else.

Apparently, he'd caught the culprits just about to jimmy the locked door.

"I wonder what they thought they'd get out of there," Reed said to Shep. The dog barked back, still anxious to chase his quarry.

Reed thought about the equipment in the shed. The riding mower was stored in there, along with some tools and other garden supplies. He usually kept an empty gas can in there to use to refuel the lawn mowers. Maybe whoever it was wanted to get some free gas.

"Strange," Reed told Shep as they circled the yard. "We've never had burglaries or vandalism on this place before."

But someone was stirring things up now. The campfires in the pastures, the damaged and broken fences all along the highway, and now this.

Someone was trespassing on the Big M and on his land, too. And Reed aimed to find out who that someone was.

Chapter Ten

April finished helping Lynette turn her father, so they could change the sheets and give him a sponge bath. He hadn't responded to their touch or their words in days. He was beyond eating or taking in fluids. All the equipment and machines had long ago been removed from his room.

Now it was just a matter of time.

Tucking the fresh-smelling sheet over his clean pajamas, April leaned down to kiss him. "Okay, Daddy, you're all set for the day. You might have some visitors today. Uncle Richard's scheduled to arrive. He's going to stay a few days, help us out around here."

Stu's breath barely left his chest. His skin was wrinkled and spotted with age. His hair, once thick and crisp brown, now consisted of a few grayed wisps.

"He looks at peace, honey," Lynette said, shaking her head at April. "I think he's ready to make his journey home."

April hated hearing that, but seeing her father this way, she would almost welcome such peace for him. For his soul. "I hope…I hope he's having pleasant dreams."

Lynette came around the bed and patted her hand. "I reckon he's making his way to your mother's side right now. She'll be there to greet him, you know. Her and your grandparents, everyone who's gone on ahead of him."

April swallowed back the hot tears burning at her throat. "That should bring me some comfort, shouldn't it?"

"It should," Lynette replied. "But death is hard on the living. We have to stay behind, missing them. I guess you've missed your mother for a long time now."

"More than I can say," April replied, weariness overtaking her as she swayed against the bed.

She was so tired, she felt chilly and numb, and a bit disoriented. When she wasn't sitting here by her father's side, she barricaded herself inside his big office on the other side of the house, going through files and calling ranch workers for reports. The work was endless, and supervising it had taught her much more than she'd ever learned growing up here.

She'd also been in touch with her department at Satire, hoping to clear up the mess with Fairchild's. And she was still trying to reach Danny Pierson. She'd left her cell phone and home numbers with his secretary, but Danny was playing hard to reach. Why he'd pick now of all times to stall out on this deal was beyond April's comprehension. But Danny had always been a grandstanding, arrogant businessman. At first, his assertiveness and confidence had attracted her. Now they repelled her. There was healthy ambition, and then there was ruthless ambition. April appreciated the first but no longer wanted to be a part of the latter.

She decided she didn't have the energy to worry about that right now. Danny knew how to reach her, and he knew what she wanted to talk to him about. He'd always been good at tracking *her* down when he wanted something.

She turned as the door creaked open. Flora stuck her head inside. "I'm sorry to interrupt, April. But Mr. Reed needs to speak with you."

April nodded, then turned back to touch her father's hand. "I'll be back in a little while, Daddy."

She came out of the dark room, her eyes hurting at the brightness of the morning. She'd lost track of the days. They'd all started merging into one big dark vortex of longing and prayer, coupled with late hours of work and bedside visits. She rarely left her father's side, rarely left the house even to go outside, unless one of the workers needed her advice on something. She had to be there with him, coaxing him to go to her mother, telling him it would be okay, telling him that God would take him home.

Lord, let him find his way back to her and You.

She saw Reed at the end of the long hallway. "Hi," was all she could manage to muster.

"Hey there. You look exhausted."

"Thanks, so do you."

"Yeah, well, I guess neither of us is getting much sleep."

"I have my reasons, but what about you?" she asked, puzzled by the serious expression on his face. "What now?" she asked, sensing that something else had happened.

"The vandalism," he replied. "It's getting worse. Had someone snooping around my garden shed two nights ago."

"Really? Why didn't you tell me sooner?"

He looked toward the closed door of the

bedroom. "You know why. Anyway, Daddy and I have been patrolling the ranch at night. We take shifts with some of the other hands."

"Thank you," April replied, not sure whether to be appreciative or angry that he'd taken matters into his own hands. "You don't have to do that, though. We can call the sheriff."

"I don't mind," he responded, scooting her out onto the dappled tiles of the long back patio. "C'mon. You need some fresh air."

"I think I've forgotten what that is."

"All the more reason to sit in the sunshine."

She did that, finding a wrought-iron patio chair to fall against. The soft floral cushions were warm and welcoming, just like Reed's gentle eyes. "Tell me all about this trespassing and vandalism."

"It's the strangest thing," Reed began, only to be interrupted by Flora at the door with lemon cookies and freshly brewed iced tea. *"Gracias,"* he told her with a big smile.

April didn't miss the smile or the way Reed had so thoughtfully asked for refreshments. "Thank you," she told him when Flora had gone back inside.

"Eat a cookie," he suggested, shoving one in her hand.

She took a bite, felt it begin to stick and grow in her tight throat, then grabbed her glass of tea. "Talk," she said, motioning with her hand.

"Oh, as I was saying, they don't take anything on these nightly excursions. And they don't do much damage. Just seems to be kids having parties on our property. Now, why they'd want anything from me—that's what I don't get."

"Have you actually caught anyone?"

"No, no. We can't seem to place where they're coming in. They move around a lot, so it's hard to pinpoint 'em. But we always find traces, can tell that they've been on the property. They don't even try to hide the messes they leave."

"So what can we do?"

"Well, I'm going back out tonight. And I've told Richard all about it. He's going on rounds with me tonight, too."

April was too tired and worried to get mad that Reed was going over her head to her uncle. After all, she had no right to question his actions or his motives. Uncle Richard had been helping out with the daily routine of this ranch for several years now.

"Well, just be careful," she said, hoping her tone didn't sound too irritated. "I can't deal with something happening to you or Uncle Richard on top of everything else." She shrugged, threw down the cookie, and looked away from his questioning gaze. "I've got this problem at work I'm trying to deal with, and no one will return my calls on that. And Daddy is getting worse by the minute. I don't know—"

He shifted forward then, taking her hand. "You know you can lean on me."

She could only nod, staring out at the tranquil flow of the swimming pool. She blinked back tears. "Look at this place. It's so beautiful. The sun is still shining. The land is thriving, growing, changing, providing. This place provides for all of us. Why did it take me so long to understand that? And to see just exactly how much work goes into a place I've taken for granted all my life? Why now, Reed, when he's dying? Why couldn't I see what he saw, what you tried to show me?"

"Hush," Reed said as he dropped to his knees and put his hands on her face. "Hush, now. It's gonna be all right."

She pushed away from him and got up to pace. "It will never be all right again, Reed. My mother is dead. My father is dying. I've made such a mess of things. I don't have any immediate family left."

"You have me." He was there, urging her to be still. "Hold on to me," he said. "Hold on or hit me or scream at me. But don't push me away again, April."

She bit her lip, trying to hold back the pain. But she was so very tired. So she turned to him, fell against him, let him wrap her in that same warmth the sun was providing.

He felt as strong and formidable as this land. He felt like the earth and the sky and the wind all wrapped up in one comforting, gentle blanket of warmth. She wondered what it would feel like to have such assurance, such security with her always. To have Reed holding her at night when she was afraid, to have him there with her each morning with the sun shining so brightly. Could she even dream of such a hope?

I am with you always.

The words from the Bible verse echoed in her head.

The Lord was with her, April realized. But did the Lord have enough grace to give her a second chance?

Always.

She looked up at Reed, saw the assurance there in his eyes. "I need…I need you," she said, the words husky and thick with tears. "I need you, Reed."

"I'm here, darlin'. I'm right here."

She let him hold her while she cried. Then she raised her head and smiled as she sniffed back tears. "You were right. I did need some fresh air."

"Want me to come in and sit with you and your daddy for a while?"

She thought about that. She hadn't allowed others inside her father's room with her. She'd wanted to be alone. But this morning, she needed some company and some comfort. "Would you?"

"Of course."

She took his hand and turned toward the house. Then she turned around and grabbed her half-eaten cookie. "Thank you again," she told him as they went back inside. "For everything."

Reed squeezed her hand and guided her back to her father's side.

They sat there with Stuart until Flora came in to tell April that her Uncle Richard had arrived and lunch was ready in the kitchen.

"Thank you," April said, her voice hoarse, her throat tight. "We'll be there in a minute."

She turned to Reed. He'd sat here without complaining, without idle small talk. He'd barely said two words, but he'd held her father's hand the whole time. And her hand. He'd held her hand. He was holding it now.

"Will you stay for lunch?" she asked, wondering when she'd decided to quit fighting her feelings for him. Suddenly, instead of wanting to avoid him, she wanted him here beside her. Was it a sign of weakness or a sign of acceptance? She couldn't be sure.

"I'll stay," he said in a soft whisper. "It'll give me a chance to update Richard."

She nodded. "Let's go get Lynette to relieve us then. She's doing Daddy's laundry, I think."

"She's a good nurse. Goes beyond the call of duty."

"Yes, she is. At first, I wasn't so sure about her. But she's very devoted to Daddy."

"We all are," Reed added as they left the room. "I'll go find Lynette while you greet your uncle."

"Okay."

April watched as he headed toward the other end of the house, where the combination laundry room and mud porch was located behind the garage. She turned left into the kitchen.

"Uncle Richard!"

Her handsome uncle turned and gave her a bittersweet smile. "C'mere, girl, and give your ol' uncle a hug."

April rushed into his arms, her breath leaving her body in the big bear hug he gave her. Uncle Richard smelled of spice and leather, which only reminded her of her father.

"It's so good to see you," she told him as she managed to extract herself from his embrace. "And you're just in time for lunch."

"Can I go in and see Stu first?"

"Of course." She glanced over at Flora,

then back to her uncle. "But I have to warn you. He doesn't look the same as you probably remember."

"I understand," Uncle Richard said, his dark eyes going misty. "I'll be right back."

While he hurried toward the back of the house, April helped Flora put ice in the tea glasses. Together, they set the table and got the food dished up. Reed came in and poured the tea, as natural and comfortable here as he would be in his own house.

Uncle Richard came back a few minutes later, his eyes watery, shock creasing his tanned face. "Hate to see him like this. You know, he was always our big brother. We could turn to Stu for anything, anything at all, and he'd move heaven and earth to see that we got it. Just wish I could do the same for him now."

"I know." April glanced from her uncle to Reed, then pushed at the salt-and-pepper tuft of curls falling across Richard's forehead in a rakish style. "Have you heard from Uncle James?"

Richard shrugged, shifting his weight, and stomped his handmade snakeskin boots. "Your other uncle is not available right now. Taking a cruise down to the Keys on the Maxwell yacht. I've sent him word, but I've yet to hear back from him."

"Some things never change," April said, amazed that the middle brother of the Maxwell clan could be so shiftless and uncaring, considering they'd all been raised by wonderful parents with a strong set of values. Uncle James and his wife, Elsie, liked the good life. And they'd taken advantage of all the Maxwell holdings in three counties to make sure they had a grand lifestyle. While they'd lived that lifestyle, Summer had spent most of her time with her mother's parents, in a house that had been standing for over a hundred years. Even though her grandparents had loved her with a strong foundation of faith, Summer had an empty place in her heart, a place still waiting to be filled by her parents. An empty place and a bitterness the size of Texas.

"What exactly does James do?" Reed asked. "I mean, when he's not traveling around."

"He's supposed to be in charge of our oil leases," Richard said as they all sat down to eat. "But I have to stay on him all the time. I've got people in place to make sure things are handled, if you get my drift."

Reed nodded, shooting a glance at April. "April's been checking the books here at the ranch. Everything seems to be in order now. April's done a good job of catching things up. Stuart has a lot of people working on the details of the day to day activities."

Richard nodded his approval. "Stu always was thorough. Now, James...he just wants to keep having a good ol' time. I've tried to tell him his rodeo days are over and he's not getting any younger, but that boy won't listen to reason. He should be here with Stu."

No wonder Summer rarely talked to her

parents. April remembered how they'd left Summer behind in the small town of Athens, Texas, time and again, so they could travel the world and be seen at all the right places, cashing in on the lucrative endorsements Uncle James had made during the heyday of his rodeo career.

How could they do that to their daughter? How could Uncle James stay away now, when his brother needed him?

"Do you think he'll come home at all?" she asked Richard after they'd said grace over the food.

"Who knows?" Richard said, shaking his head as he took a corn pone from the basket Flora had put on the table. "Flora, honey, you've outdone yourself. Fresh peas and fried chicken, mashed potatoes. Gayle will have my hide for going off my diet, but I can't resist."

Flora beamed with pride. *"Gracias."*

"Flora, sit down and join us," April said, urging the woman down into a chair. "Where's Horaz today?"

Flora looked embarrassed. "In town with Tomás. Taking care of some business."

"Oh, okay." April figured that business had to do with the traffic ticket Tomás had been issued. "I hope everything works out."

"*Sí,*" Flora replied as she absently dipped herself a big helping of steaming peas. Then she gave Richard a bright smile. "Teenagers."

"Tell me about it," Richard said, laughing. "These girls—remember them, Flora? Growing up here on the Big M and running loose all around half of Texas. We sure had our hands full, didn't we?"

"*Sí,*" Flora said again, grinning. "And how is Autumn? She is a good girl, that one."

April smiled as she sampled the creamy mashed potatoes. Everyone loved Autumn, even if her cousin was a bit set in her ways and as straitlaced as an old shoe.

Uncle Richard chewed his chicken, then laughed. "Autumn is still Autumn. Born with a calculator attached to her hand. Always after the bottom line, that one. Have you talked to her lately, April?"

"Only on e-mail," April admitted. "I haven't made many phone calls to New York. I'm usually in with Daddy and I don't want to disturb him. But Summer and Autumn e-mail me daily, and me, them. They've offered to come down, but I told them not yet."

"Modern technology. I'll never get the hang of it," Uncle Richard said. "In fact, I'll let y'all be the first to know a big secret. I'm retiring in the fall."

April put down her fork. "You're closing the firm?"

"Nah, now, I'll never close Maxwell Financial Group. We've got clients all over Texas, honey. But I've hired me a hotshot financial advisor to take over. He knows all about computers and technology, and he's as sharp as a tack when it comes to making people money. The man is a genius."

"Have you told Autumn about this?" April asked, wondering how her cousin would take her father's retirement.

Autumn had always had this dream of one day returning to Atlanta, Texas, to work with her father. But her father probably didn't know about Autumn's dream, since Autumn refused to stray from her ten-year plan. And that plan included working in New York for a few more years.

"Not yet," Richard admitted. "Your Aunt Gayle knows, of course. And I've already put Campbell on the payroll—that's one of the reasons I was able to come here to be with y'all. Campbell can hold down the fort."

"You hired this…Campbell to take your place?"

"Not necessarily. He will be chief financial advisor, but I'll always be the boss, retired or not. Campbell Dupree understands how things work. He won't be any trouble for the family. None at all. He grew up in Louisiana, but he got a top-notch education at Harvard. He's traveled the world, got a real handle on how international finances work."

Richard said this with the kind of pride

and confidence that April's daddy used to exude. The Maxwell men were nothing if not arrogant and self-assured. She had to wonder if Campbell Dupree fit that mold, too. And how Autumn would react to such a man taking over the family business.

"Maybe you should tell her, Uncle Richard," April said with a gentle plea. "I mean, she's going to be so surprised."

"Well, I don't know why. That girl knows I can't work the rest of my life. If James can travel the world without a care, then why can't I?"

"You deserve some downtime, that's true," April replied, "but Autumn—well, she cut her teeth at Maxwell Financial Group. She sat at your knee, right there in the company you built from the ground up, and learned everything she needed to know about money and finances."

"That's right and one day, it will all be hers," Uncle Richard reasoned. He dipped more peas and grabbed another corn pone.

"She might be upset that you've hired someone though."

"Now, why?" Uncle Richard sent April a sharp look. "Unless you're trying to tell me that Autumn might have wanted the job."

"Well, she's hinted that she'd love to one day move back home and—"

"Well, bless Bessy, why didn't the girl tell me that?"

"It's not set in stone," April said, hoping Autumn wouldn't be angry at her for spilling this secret goal. "I guess she's just afraid of...of disappointing you. You know, if something went wrong."

She glanced over at Flora and Reed, but found no help there. Flora kept her eyes glued to her plate and Reed tried hard not to look too curious and amused.

Uncle Richard stared across the table at her. "Autumn could never disappoint me. She's my baby. I'm so proud of her. You know, she's sent some big clients my way over the years. That girl's got contacts all over the world. She's about the only person who could match Campbell, I reckon."

"She's very good at her job, that's for sure," April said, pushing her fork around in her food.

"Well, Sam Houston and Custer, too," Uncle Richard said as he sat, shock-faced. "You just never know about people. I'll have to think about this and see what I can do."

"Well, you can't fire your new hotshot financial genius," April said. "That wouldn't be right."

"No, that wouldn't do," her uncle agreed. "The man's got an ironclad contract. But I might have another solution." He beamed at April, then winked. "A solution that just might be a win-win situation for all of us."

April wondered what her lovable but impulsive uncle had suddenly concocted for his only daughter. Maybe she should warn Autumn. Later, she decided. Much later. Right now, she didn't have time to get caught in the middle of a family squabble. And right now, Autumn was deeply and gleefully caught up in tax season.

She'd find the right time to explain things to her stubborn cousin. But much later.

Chapter Eleven

"Did you ever find out what your uncle has cooked up?"

Reed asked April later that night.

"No. He's as stubborn and tough as an old barnyard rooster, and just as unpredictable."

"Do you think Autumn's gonna pitch a fit about him retiring and hiring this new fellow?"

"Oh, yes," April said. "I guess I should warn her, but honestly, I don't have the energy right now to handle putting out yet another family fire."

"It's between them, anyway," Reed said. "Might be best to let Richard tell her."

"I thought about that, but I can't keep this from Autumn. We tell each other everything. I just have to find the right time to break it to her," she whispered back, careful not to bother her father.

Not that their quiet chatter could bother him. He hadn't responded to anything they said. His body was slowly shutting down. So now April could only wait and pray.

So many people had been by to see him. April had tried to keep a list of everyone, so she could thank all of them later.

"You have a remarkable family," Reed said, his words soft-spoken. "You know, when we were growing up, there was this one big old oak tree right near the back fence of y'all's yard. I used to climb up in that tree and watch—"

"You spied on me?"

He shook his head. "Not spying so much. Remember those grand parties your parents would have out on the back lawn?"

"Oh, yes. Mother loved entertaining, loved having a crowd here. Sometimes, she'd have the whole Cattle Baron's Ball committee here for a 'planning' party. They loved attending that big event, mingling with all the other ranchers and oil people. Of course, I had to decline Daddy's invitation to the ball this year, even though Flora said I should go in his place." April stared at her father, then asked, "So, you wanted to come to the parties?"

Reed nodded. "I wanted to be a part of something big like that. But it wasn't the glittery parties I wanted to see." He turned in the muted light, his gaze falling across April's face, washing her in longing. "It was you."

April felt the heat of her blush down to her toes. "But you saw me every day, Reed. We ran around this entire ranch like a couple of wild heathens."

"I know that," he said, and she could see the memories in his eyes. "But at those parties… you'd walk out, all dressed up in fluffy party gowns and I'd just about fall out of that tree." He shrugged. "I reckon somewhere around my fourteenth birthday, I started seeing you as a real live girl. I remember the party your parents had for you when you turned sixteen."

"You were invited to that party, Reed Garrison."

"I know I was. And I came."

"But you didn't stay," April said, the memories rushing over her, reminding her of that warm spring night years ago. She remembered seeing Reed in his church suit. He'd looked so uncomfortable, and so very handsome. And she remembered the way he'd looked at her. "I wore a white dress."

"It was the most beautiful thing."

"You wouldn't talk to me. I thought you were mad about something."

"I wasn't mad. I wanted to kiss you."

"But you were afraid?"

"Very afraid."

"You acted so funny, as if you had a frog in your throat."

"I did. I saw you through the open doors, and then you came down the back verandah stairs in that white dress and your mother's pearls. I'd already lost my heart to you, but that night, I knew something was different. That things would be different between us if I did kiss you."

"Oh, Reed—"

Stuart moaned, causing both of them to jump up as if they'd been caught.

"Daddy?"

April felt her father's hand squeezing hers. "I think he wants to tell us something, Reed."

"Stuart? It's Reed. What is it?"

Stuart moaned again, lifted his other hand.

"Daddy, do you hurt? Can I get you anything?"

Both Reed and April leaned forward, trying to hear the raspy words. But April heard only one word.

"Happy."

She looked up at Reed. "Did I hear him right?"

Reed glanced back down at Stuart with a frown. "You're happy?" he asked.

Stuart nodded, a slight movement of his head. He didn't open his eyes. "For you two."

Then he fell back into the deep sleep April had become so used to seeing.

Reed motioned April to follow him to the door. "Uh, April…I think he believes we're, uh—"

"Back together," she finished. "I didn't think he could hear anything we say, but I guess he can."

"And we've said a lot lately."

"But we never said we were back together."

Reed pulled her close, planting a soft kiss on her cheek. "Some things don't need to be voiced to be seen, April."

Shocked, she could only stare up at him. Could her father, as sick as he was, see what she couldn't admit with her own heart? "I don't know—"

"I do," Reed replied. "But I don't have time to go into this now, and besides, I can tell you're not ready for it yet. I have to meet Richard down at the stables. We're going out on patrol, remember?"

"Yes. Flora was supposed to wake him at ten. Is it that late?"

"Yes, it is. Why don't you go to bed and let Lynette take over?"

"I will in a little while. I'm just going to sit with him a little longer. See if he says anything else."

Reed gave her a soft grin. "Stuart believes in us, April. Maybe you should try doing that, too."

April watched him saunter up the hallway, her heart drumming a beat of longing and pride. Her father hadn't been able to talk to her very much, but he'd told her all the things that were important. He loved her, and he was happy to see her back with Reed. Her dying father believed she was home for good and everything was as it should be.

Why couldn't she believe that, too?

* * *

"I don't believe you finally took the time to call me," April said into the phone an hour later. "Danny, do you know what time it is here in Texas?"

"I know exactly what time it is," Danny Pierson said into the phone, his tone smug and pleasant. "That's because I'm sitting in a hotel in downtown Dallas."

"You're in Dallas?" April moved through the house, the mobile phone at her ear. She'd left Lynette with her father so she could take this call. "What are you doing there?"

"Checking up on our store at the Galleria," Danny said. "It's one of our top producers, you know."

"I've heard things weren't going so well with Fairchild's," April shot back, unwilling to deal with his spin on things.

"There are always rumors in our business. You should know that, April."

"Why are you blocking our contracts

with Fairchild's, Danny? It's a bit late in the game to shut things down now."

"I'm just concerned," Danny replied. "This is a risky move for Satire. And it's even more risky for Fairchild's. You know how exclusive our stores are, April."

"Yes, I do. That's why I think this is a good move. Satire will bring in hordes of customers. You have to agree with that. Fairchild's certainly knew that when these contracts were being negotiated."

"Yes, but I didn't work for Fairchild's then. And that was—well, that was when I thought I could trust you."

"You can trust me now, Danny, past differences aside. Don't do this. Just because *we* didn't work out, don't make this personal."

"Is that what you think I'm doing?"

"That's it exactly," she said, fatigue making her snap. "And I really don't have time to go into that now. Just know that our contract is tight and you can't back out on the deal now."

"Meet me in Dallas and we'll go over the details."

"I can't do that. My father is very ill."

"I'm sorry to hear that. Your family has quite an impressive name around these parts, highly respected. I know this is hard on you."

"Very hard. Which is why I don't need this problem with Fairchild's right now. Just back off and honor the original agreement, Danny."

"Only if you meet me to discuss it."

"I can't do that."

"Then I'll drive up to Paris. It's not that far from Dallas. I checked the map. Always did want to see that replica of the Eiffel Tower with the red cowboy hat on top you always talked about. Didn't you tell me it's near the Civic Center?"

"Don't come here," April said, panic bubbling through her system. "It's not a good time."

"But business is business and I'm sure you don't want this deal to go sour."

"Danny, my father is dying. Just do what

you can to make this happen. I can't worry about this right now."

"We'll see," Danny replied, his tone less threatening now. "I understand about your father, April. I'll try to go back to the board of directors and see what I can do to clear this problem. But I'd like to see you."

"Another time," April said. "Just call me tomorrow with the details."

She hung up, then glanced out the big windows at the back of the house, a sense of dread filling her soul as the night grew dark and cloudy. She did not need Danny Pierson here, harassing her about business or personal matters. Not now.

So much to worry about. Her father. Reed and Uncle Richard out there hunting down trespassers. Danny and business pushing at her. So much to think about, to take care of.

"I need You, Lord. I need Your strength."

She waited, staring out into the dark night. But the silence of an empty, desolate house was her only answer. That and a distance rumble of thunder and lightning out over the trees to the west.

April turned from the darkness and walked down the long hall toward her father's room.

"Mighty quiet night," Richard said as he adjusted the black Stetson over his wiry salt-and-pepper hair. "Too quiet. But looks like a little bit of rain might blow in."

"Yep," Reed answered in a whisper. "Maybe if a storm comes, our vandals will give up this game for tonight."

"I doubt that," Richard replied, chuckling. "If it's kids out for kicks, they won't know when to quit. Probably don't have sense enough to get in out of the rain."

"Until we catch 'em," Reed said. "Then they'll have more to worry about than wet clothes. Want some more coffee?"

"Nah. I'm getting too old for all that caffeine. I tell you, son, old age ain't no picnic."

"I hear that." Reed was silent for a

while, then added, "Stu spoke to April and me tonight."

"He did? Well, that's something, I reckon."

"He said he was happy. For us."

Richard let out a grunt that merged with another rumble of thunder in the sky. "A dying man's last wish. He wants you and April together. He's always wanted that."

"He's not the only one."

"When are you gonna make that happen, son?"

"That all depends on April."

"How's that gonna work, with you here and her back in New York?"

"You think she'll go back?"

"Well, I'm thinking she has a life there. No need for her to waste away on this old ranch, unless, of course, that's what she wants to do."

"It'll be her choice."

"So you'll let her go again?"

"I don't want her to stay here and resent me for it."

"What about if she stays here and loves you for it?"

"Now that would be a different matter."

"You need to learn the fine art of persuasion, Reed."

"I'm not a salesman like you, Richard. I don't have the right words."

"Oh, I think you do. I can talk a good game myself, as far as people's finances. But when it comes to understanding women—"

"Zero?"

"You got it. But I do know this. You have to persuade women sometimes. They want to be wooed. They want to know they're loved and treasured. They like security."

"You sound just like my daddy. He pretty much told me the very same thing. By my reasoning, April should see that she'd be secure with me."

"Women like that old-fashioned kind of romance," Richard replied sagely. "Why, I don't know. But Gayle is always telling me that. So I romance her as often as I can, just to be on the safe side."

"April is a modern woman, Richard. She

has a mind of her own. She's very independent. And very secure in her own way. I'm not so sure romance can compete with that."

"Maybe not. But I think she loves you just as much as you love her. She just needs some reassurance."

"Don't we all?"

"Yes, we do. That's why we have to keep the faith, through good and bad."

They fell silent again. Reed could hear the cicadas singing, the fluttering melody of the alfalfa swaying in the damp wind. He smelled a hint of honeysuckle, reminding him of April's sweet-smelling hair. He closed his eyes in a prayer—not his will, but God's plan.

And then he heard the snapping of trees, the crackle of heat against branches, and he smelled a different kind of scent, this one acrid and smoky. He saw the fire rising up out of the copse of bow dark trees nestled along the fence rail.

"Richard?"

"I see it. Somebody's gone and set fire to that wooden gate out there."

Reed hopped up. "With this wind, that could spread to the fields."

"I'm right behind you," Richard shouted as they rushed toward the growing fire.

Too late to worry about an ambush or a surprise attack. Whoever was doing this had grown bolder. And much more dangerous.

"Hey!" Reed called as two shadowy figures took off running through the trees. "Hey, stop right there!"

"Did you bring a rifle?" Richard shouted as he stomped at the fire. He took off the lightweight jacket he was wearing and hit at the trees.

"I did," Reed answered as he searched the trees. "But I left it in the truck. I didn't think things would turn this nasty."

"Go after them," Richard called. "I'll get this little brushfire out in no time."

"You sure?" Reed asked, stepping on embers and hitting at the fence with a broken tree limb.

"Yeah. It's almost out now."

Richard was right. They'd managed to subdue the fire that had been leaping up the fence and through the small trees. And thankfully, Reed felt a few big, fat raindrops hitting his hot skin.

Rain. God had sent rain.

I think it's going to rain.

April typed the words on her laptop, careful to keep an eye on the nearby bed and her silent, sleeping father.

She continued the e-mail to her cousins in New York.

Things are getting tough here. Summer, I appreciate your trying to get away, but I understand when things come up. You are needed at the center, so please don't worry about rushing down here. You both will be here soon enough, I know. And you'll be here when I need you. And I will need you. Reed has been so sweet. He sat with Daddy and me tonight. He sat and held my father's hand and prayed and talked to me in soothing, comforting words. I've changed since coming home. I now know that this is home. But I'm still afraid of making that final commitment—to Reed and the future he could offer me. I want to love him. I do love him. And I need him now more than ever. But I'm so tired and so afraid. I'm afraid to love him. Isn't that the silliest thing? I can see him reaching out to me, can feel his eyes on me. But it's as if I can't move toward him, as if something is holding me back. My heart is too heavy to hold all the feelings I have for Reed.

She stopped typing and closed her eyes to that heaviness for a brief moment. Then she finished the e-mail. I'll talk to y'all later. I'm going to sit here and wait for Reed and Uncle Richard to come back.

She shut the laptop and stilled, listening

to the wind and the thunder, her gaze moving over her father's shadowy profile.

Then she closed her eyes again and fell asleep, her dreams lost in a gossamer time of happiness and laughter, a time of a young boy in his church suit and a young girl in her white dress and pearls, smiling at each other on a perfect spring night.

April heard the rain hitting the roof at about the same time she heard something crashing on the other side of the house.

Jumping up in disoriented, wide-eyed shock, she checked on her father, then stumbled across the room and creaked open the door of the bedroom. "Lynette?"

No answer. Flora and Horaz had gone home right after dinner. And April had sent Lynette to bed down the hall hours ago. Glancing back at the digital bedside clock, she saw that it was well past midnight.

She called out again, afraid Lynette had fallen. "Is anyone there?"

The rain came down in a wash of gray that danced across the yard like a sheet waltzing in the wind. The sky lit up with the glare of brilliant golden lightning and the banging of angry thunder. She watched it through the many windows around the patio, her breath coming in little shallow gasps as she stayed in her spot at the bedroom door.

Worried that something had happened to Lynette, April decided she couldn't just hover here like a ninny. She hurried toward the front of the house, hoping to find the nurse. "Lynette, are you all right?"

And that's when April saw the figure of a man standing at the other end of the hall.

Chapter Twelve

April squinted into the darkness, thinking maybe Reed and Richard had returned. But she could tell by the stance of the intruder and by the hooded jacket he wore to hide his face that this wasn't either of those two men.

The locked gun cabinet was behind the intruder, in her father's office, and her cell phone was upstairs in her bedroom. No help there. She didn't dare go back in the bedroom. The intruder might follow her there and hurt her father.

Trying to think which way to go and

what to do next, April called out. "What do you want?"

"I won't hurt you," the man said, his voice shaky and raspy. "I just need to get some stuff and leave."

"What do you want?" April asked again, moving back toward the front of the house. If she could run up the central hall to the front door, she'd be able to grab a phone or escape. But she couldn't leave her father alone.

"Just turn around and go back in your daddy's room."

Surprised, April realized this intruder knew the layout of the house—and apparently knew *her.* As her eyes adjusted to the darkness, she saw that the man was dressed in dark clothes, making it hard to even guess at his identity. "Who are you?"

"Just go back inside the room and you won't get hurt."

He had a Spanish accent.

April felt the hair on the back of her neck standing up. "What are you after?"

"Lady, you ask way too many questions." He waved his hand at her and advanced toward her. "I don't want to hurt you."

"Then just leave. Now." She hoped he didn't have a weapon. "No one will have to know you were even here. But you need to hurry. My uncle will be back soon."

He fidgeted and glanced around behind him. "I can't do that."

He sounded resigned to his dirty work.

And he sounded young and frightened.

April moved a step closer, determined to get him away from the back of the house and her father. She checked again, squinting in the darkness, but still didn't see any type of weapon on him. And then she looked around for one of her own.

Because she wasn't going to let whoever this was get away. Not without a fight, at least.

Reed ran through the rain like a man being chased by hounds. He could see one of the vandals just up ahead. Apparently, this time they'd hidden their means of escape near the very back of the property line, probably on one of the riding trails.

"Stop," Reed called, his words lost in the wind and the rain. "You'll only make this worse if you keep running."

Whoever it was kept right on running anyway. Reed hurried after them, his bum knee sending signals of protest with each step.

They were nearing the fence along the property line now. The pasture gave way to uneven, weather-worn gullies and terraces. Reed hopped over a muddy terrace, the rain falling in his eyes and blinding him. He winced as his leg twisted, but he didn't stop.

The lone figure hesitated just enough at the fence line to give Reed an edge. He surged forward with all the power of a linebacker, tackling the man in a groan of pain and exertion just as he tried to climb over the fence.

They rolled and tussled in the wet mud

and grass, but Reed had more strength and muscle than the other guy. It took Reed only a few seconds to realize this wasn't even a grown man.

He was wrestling with a kid.

April said a prayer, hoping that her father would sleep through the ruckus and that Lynette was safe in her room. "Just take what you want and leave," she said, watching the shadowy figure for any signs of flight or fight.

"I don't want to hurt anyone."

The man—make that *boy*—seemed jittery and skittish, but then he was breaking and entering her house, so she figured that gave him the right to be a little nervous. It also gave her an edge.

"That's good that you don't want to hurt me." She stood perfectly still, her gaze fluttering over a huge clay vase sitting on a dark console in the center of the hallway. If she could get to that vase…

He didn't speak, didn't move.

"So are we just going to stand here all night?" she asked, her breath sticking in her throat.

"No, I don't think so."

"Good. Just turn around and leave the way you came and we'll call it even. Please, I don't want to disturb my father."

"I can't do that."

"Why not?"

The dark figure stalked toward her, his hand held out. "C'mon, my friend is waiting by the road. You'll have to come with me."

"Got you," Reed said as he landed his quarry flat on his back, mud and rain sliding off both of them. He held the captive down with both hands, his breath coming in a great rush of air. "Now you can explain what you're doing on Maxwell land," Reed shouted.

The kid kept his face turned away. And he wasn't talking.

Reed grabbed him by the chin, turned him around, and in a flash of lightning saw the face he would have least expected to be doing damage to the Big M.

"Tomás?"

The boy winced, closed his eyes, then moaned. "Let me up, Reed. So I can explain. Before it's too late."

"What do you mean, too late?" Reed said, loosening his grip on the boy.

"The house," Tomás hollered. "They went to the big house. I don't want them to hurt April."

Reed held the boy by his shirt collar. "Who? Who's up at the house?"

"My friends. Two of them. They had this plan—to take money from the safe—that's all we wanted, just some money."

Reed's blood went cold as realization hit him. "So you planned this whole thing? You distracted everyone just so they could break in?"

"*Sí,*" Tomás said, his voice shaky, his expression filled with shame and remorse.

"You messed with the wrong people, son," Reed said angrily. Then he yanked

Tomás up and half dragged him along, mud sluicing at their feet as he hurried back to his truck. "You'd better hope it's not too late, Tomás. You'd better pray that nothing's happened at that house."

"I'm not going anywhere with you," April said, her pulse throbbing at an alarming rate in her ear. But she refused to be afraid. Suddenly, everything was very clear in her mind. This was her home, and that was her father lying in that bed. She'd been afraid of loving Reed too much; she'd been afraid of coming home to death and grief. But she wasn't afraid now. She wasn't about to let this little twerp get the best of her. "Did you hear me? I'm not leaving this house with you."

He shifted his feet, his gaze darting here and there. "Look, I don't want any trouble. We'll just drive you out to the highway and let you go."

"You said, there's someone with you?"

"He's waiting in the car. But I promise

we won't hurt you. We don't want any trouble. We just wanted some easy cash. This was supposed to be easy."

She breathed a sigh of relief at his words, but didn't believe him. "Well, this is not easy for either of us, is it? My father is very ill, but then, you probably already know that. And yet, you still just wanted some easy cash? Does it make you feel good, breaking into the home of a dying man?"

"I'm sorry," he said, his head bent. "It wasn't supposed to be like this—"

April listened, her heart skipping and skidding. This was just a kid! And his voice seemed so familiar.

This new knowledge made her bold, took away some of her initial shock and fear. She stared at the stranger, thinking it was time to end this standoff. Making a split-second decision, she rushed for the table to grab the vase.

But the kid was faster. He ran smack into her and pushed at her grasping hand. April caught hold of the lip of the heavy vase, then aimed it for his head. He ducked, but not before she managed to lift the vase just enough to nick his temple with a hard blow. Screaming, he grasped at her hand, sending the vase crashing to the tile floor. The echo of the crash startled the kid, giving April time to push him away. Expecting him to come at her, she quickly grabbed a fractured piece of the broken clay to use as a weapon. But the boy backed away, then turned and ran up the wide hall.

And right into Lynette Proctor.

Reed and Richard both rushed inside the gaping door leading from Stuart's office to the back verandah.

"Somebody sure broke in," Richard said, his breath heaving, his hair plastered with rain and mud.

Reed pushed Tomás ahead of him, careful to keep a firm grip on the teenager's wet, dirty clothes. "Yeah, but then, our friend here had already told us that." He gave the frightened kid another shove as they entered the house. Tomás had talked a lot in his nervousness. And Reed still couldn't believe what the boy had told them.

But now, he saw it with his own eyes.

The office was ransacked, drawers left open and empty, files tossed to the four walls.

"I'll deal with this, and you, later," Reed told Tomás.

"Where is our help?" Richard whispered as they heard a commotion on the other side of the house. He headed for the gun cabinet.

"The sheriff should be sending someone," Reed said. They'd called 911 from the truck. He shoved Tomás at Richard. "Watch him."

Richard nodded toward the gun cabinet. "Don't you need protection?"

"I'll manage," Reed replied. He didn't want to accidentally shoot April or Lynette, or anyone else for that matter. "You just make sure Tomás stays put."

"Be careful," Richard said, his grip on Tomás's shirt collar making the boy grimace in pain.

Reed rushed out into the dark hallway, the sound of rain and thunder mingling with the sounds of angry voices emanating from the front of the house.

"April?" he called, a rippling fear causing him to see red. "April, are you all right?"

He ran to Stuart's room and was relieved to see that Stuart was sleeping and undisturbed.

But where was April? Where had that noise come from?

When he heard sirens out on the road, Reed sent up a prayer of thanks for that, at least. "April?"

"We're in here."

He followed her voice, hoping he wouldn't find something horrible in the next room.

He found them in the den. Lynette Proctor and April stood over the trembling figure they had cornered on a chair by the window.

"Are y'all all right?" Reed asked as he hurried to April.

"We're fine," she said, falling into his embrace and getting herself all wet in the process. "We're okay."

She sounded a bit shaken. Reed looked her over, taking in the fear and resolve in her big, dark eyes. "Are you sure?"

Lynette grunted, then held a hand toward the man in the chair. "We snared us a burglar. I tackled him right there in the hallway, after April tried to ping him with a vase."

"They tried to kill me," the teenager said, his voice shrill, his tone whining and afraid.

"You broke into my father's office," April shouted down at him. "You could have hurt someone, or worse, you could have gotten shot."

"If I'd had me a gun," Lynette said, her tone smug and firm, her eyes flashing. "I heard him rustling around in there. Left a mess, that's what he did."

Reed stared down at the dark-headed boy. "You're a friend of Tomás's, right? Adan? You're Adan."

The boy didn't answer. He just sat there glaring.

Richard came in then, pushing Tomás ahead of him. "Looks like we found our vandals." He thumped Tomás on the head. "Kid, have you lost your mind, trying to break into the Big M?"

Tomás crumpled into a heap on a nearby chair, then shot an accusing look at his partner in crime. "You told me nobody would get hurt."

"Nobody did," April said. "But you're both lucky we didn't shoot first and ask questions later."

"He was only supposed to take some cash from the safe," Tomás said, his defiance almost comical. Except this was no laughing matter.

"I couldn't find the safe," his friend

wailed. "Then she came down the hall toward me." He pointed to April, then swallowed hard. "They're gonna put us in jail, Tomás." He lapsed into Spanish.

Reed thought he heard a very sincere appeal to God in there somewhere. "You need to pray, both of you." He turned to Tomás. " Tomás, why would you be a part of this?"

Tomás shrugged. "They dared me."

"They dared you?" Richard echoed, shaking his head. "Son, haven't we been good to you?"

Tomás glared up at him. "*Sí*, but…I feel like a loser. The hired help, getting handouts. Always only handouts."

April leaned close. "Tomás, your grandparents are a part of this family. We don't give handouts. We have loyal people on our land, people who work hard and make a good living. We consider all of them family, even you." She grabbed him by the arm. "Now tell me why you did this?"

"I told you—they dared me. I had to

show them I wasn't scared. But…my ride left me out there in the pasture." He frowned at the other boy. "They were only supposed to take a little money."

Reed winced, shook his head. "You're gonna have to tell the sheriff the whole story, Tomás. And I have to call your family."

Tomás groaned. "It started out as a game. A dare. We had some fun, hanging out in the pastures. Then we started leaving things here and there, just to—"

"Just to make us think it wasn't serious," Reed finished. "I guess that's why you tried to break into my toolshed, too, right? Just to throw us off?"

"We didn't mean any harm."

Reed glanced at April. "Until someone suggested robbing the big house, huh? Then you had to distract us one more time, so your friend here could do his dirty work, right?"

Tomás glared across at the other boy. "He said it would be for kicks, to get some cash, just for fun. He said no one would ever trace it back to us."

"Are you both dumb as dirt?" Richard asked, his hand holding onto Tomás's friend with a firm grip. "What's your name again, son?"

"Adan," the boy mumbled, his head down.

"Well, Adan, I hear the sheriff coming. Might as well give me your parents' number, so we can call them, too. And whoever was waiting to give you a ride out of here—well, I reckon they're long gone by now. We'll have to let their parents know. It's gonna take a while to straighten all of this out."

Reed looked at April again. "Are you sure—"

"I'm fine," she said. "Just a bit dazed."

"You sure didn't need this."

"No, I didn't. But at least now we know who was behind the vandalism."

He nodded. "Yeah, we solved it."

"Together," she said, her smile bittersweet.

"With me out there, chasing down a kid, and you in here, trying to—what was that Lynette said?—*ping* another one on the head with a vase." He felt the shudder passing through his body. "April, when I think of what could have happened—"

"It didn't."

"At least we got through this without too much trouble, and nobody seriously hurt."

"We're quite a pair."

"Yeah," Reed said, relief flooding through his system. "Quite a pair." He couldn't tell her that he'd been in a dark fear out there, wondering if she had been hurt. He couldn't show her just how relieved he really was. "Let's go let the sheriff in and get this night over with."

"Flora, we're not going to press charges," April said the next day.

Flora was inconsolable. "*Gracias,* April, *gracias. Lo siento. Lo siento.*"

"It's not your fault," April said, taking Flora into her arms. "It's going to be all right."

"What will become of my grandson?" Flora asked, her eyes watery and red-rimmed.

"Community service," April replied. "Reed and I thought it was the best way to teach these boys a lesson."

"They could have gone to jail," Flora replied, shaking her head. "*Por qué?* Why would Tomás do such a thing?"

April had wondered that herself during the sleepless hours of the long, rainy night. "From what we could gather, his friends pressured him. They saw an opportunity and they took it. They talked Tomás into creating a distraction, so one of them could sneak into the house and get whatever cash they could find. Cash and other valuables, according to the sheriff."

"There is no excuse for this," Flora said, wiping her eyes. "His parents—they finally sat down with us and Tomás and had a long talk. At least, that is something good."

"That *is* something good," April agreed. "Maybe now they will pay more attention to Tomás."

"He might not get to play football this

fall," Flora said. "Serves him right, *el niño loco.*"

Reed came into the kitchen, followed by Horaz. "It's all taken care of," he told April.

Horaz took his wife into his arms, talking to her softly in Spanish.

"What was decided?" April asked.

"There will be a hearing, closed, because they're juveniles, of course. But from what we could gather and from what the sheriff could promise us, they'll probably have to pick up trash up on the main highway for the rest of the summer, then do volunteer work at the local food bank and a couple of other charities for a long time to come."

April nodded. "Do you think that's a fair punishment?"

Reed let out a frustrated breath. "I don't know. What they did was wrong, but in the end, nobody got hurt, thank goodness. They were more stupid and scared than dangerous. It could have been much worse."

"You're right. I don't know who was more scared last night, me or that boy."

"He came here with Tomás," Reed said, disgust evident on his face. "He had meals right here in the kitchen, swam in the pool, fished, rode horses."

"And saw a lot of things he could pawn or sell for profit," April reminded him. "Will they be on probation for a while?"

"I'd say a good long while," Reed replied. "And they're both off the football team for the next season."

"You tried to warn Tomás," she said, taking Reed's hand in hers.

"I should have done more."

"Reed, you can't take care of all of us. You're only human, you know."

"More human than I realized," he said. "My knee is still protesting my midnight run."

"I'm proud of you."

"Oh, yeah?"

She felt the heat of his gaze, the longing in his question. "Yeah."

"Proud enough to have dinner with me tonight?"

"I can't leave—"

"Here, in the dining room?"

She glanced around. "Do you think that's wise? I mean, after all the commotion last night?"

"Don't you think we deserve a nice dinner for our crime-solving abilities?"

That made her smile. "I don't know. I wouldn't feel right—"

"It's just dinner, April. Just you and me."

Confused, she stared up at him. "What do you have in mind?"

"Just some time together, alone. We'll be right here, if your dad needs us."

"Who's cooking?"

"Not me," he assured her. "And certainly not Flora. She needs some time off."

"I agree."

"My mom will provide the food."

"Reed, she's already done so much."

"She doesn't mind. It's part of her matchmaking skills."

That made her smile. "Everyone's determined to bring us together."

"And I'm the first one in line."

"Is that what this dinner is all about?"

"Maybe."

April smiled up at him. "Should I dress for this dinner?"

"Yes, ma'am. Dress up. Get all glamorous."

"For you?"

"Will you, for me?"

"I think I can find something in the back of my closet, if I can just find the energy actually to get dressed."

"Good." He leaned forward and gave her a kiss on the forehead. "You rest up and I'll see you around seven."

"Okay."

April watched as he left the room, then turned back to Flora and Horaz. They both looked miserable and embarrassed.

"It's okay," she told them as she rushed forward to give them a hug. "I love you both so much. You know that, right?"

"Sí," Horaz said. "We feel the same."

"Let's go visit Daddy," April suggested, needing to be near her father.

Taking them both by the arms, she led the old couple down the long hallway, refusing to let the scare they'd had last night bother her anymore.

She'd learned what really mattered, since she'd been back at the Big M. And right now, seeing her father and being with the people she loved was all that mattered.

And those people included Reed Garrison.

Chapter Thirteen

"Can you believe this?" Summer said as she finished reading April's latest e-mail. "Vandals and a break-in at the Big M? That's just what April needed."

"Doesn't sound too good," Autumn said absently from her paper cluttered desk. "I'm just glad everyone is okay."

"Yes," Summer said as she shut down the computer and took her empty teacup to the sink. "I'm surprised April didn't shoot that Adan."

"April hasn't been near a gun since she left Texas," Autumn reminded her overly zealous cousin.

"She still knows how to use one, though," Summer replied. "We all do."

"Don't remind me," Autumn countered. "I don't like guns."

"Necessary in today's world."

Autumn glanced up at her cousin. "You must have had a bad day at work."

Summer ran a hand through her long hair. "Yeah, if that's what you call helping three more battered women find the strength to stay away from their husbands, then I guess I did have a pretty rotten day."

Autumn dropped her ink pen. "I'm sorry you didn't get to go visit with April."

"Well, work has to come first."

"You need a vacation, Summer."

"So they tell me." She shrugged. "Let's not worry about me. Just think—right about now, Reed is getting dinner ready for April. That's so nice." Then she let out a gasp that made Autumn jump.

"What?"

"I just remembered. Today is April's birthday."

* * *

Reed figured April had forgotten that today was her birthday. But he hadn't, which was why he'd tried so hard all day to get things in order for their special dinner.

The house was back to normal. Reed had hired two ranch hands to help him get the office cleaned up. Adan hadn't found the safe, which was tucked behind a small book cabinet, but he'd done a good bit of damage. His parents had readily agreed to pay for that. All three of the boys were put on probation and community service, their parents ordered to supervise them strictly. The driver had bolted and run, but his parents had been just as upset as Tomás's and Adan's, and the authorities agreed he was just as guilty. They'd been planning this all summer by deliberately messing up the land so everyone on the ranch would be distracted just enough to allow the break-in. And they'd waited for the perfect night to do it.

It had been calculated and perfectly

timed, but they'd failed anyway, because they were young and hadn't thought of the consequences or all the things that could go wrong. Well, they'd be thinking about that for a long time to come now.

The judge had also suggested they all attend church on a regular basis. Reed didn't think that would be a problem.

He glanced around the formal dining room one more time, making sure everything was ready for his evening with April. When he thought about what might have happened last night, he thanked God for protecting April and Lynette and April's father. Things could have taken a bad turn, but that was over now and Reed was glad. He only wanted to give April some time away from all of it, a chance to put all the bad stuff out of her mind.

The long glistening pinewood table was set with the abstract sunflower-etched china and matching crystal. Two golden glazed hurricane lamps sitting on the massive sideboard sparkled with the fire of vanilla-scented candles. The big, glass-paned doors were thrown open to the tiled patio and the pool beyond, allowing the cool night breeze and the scent of fresh blooming jasmine and gardenias to waft through the big room. Soft, soothing Spanish guitar music played in the background.

"It looks real nice, son."

Turning to give his mother thanks and a hug, Reed said, "You go on home and rest now. I appreciate everything y'all did. And thanks for inviting Richard over for the evening so we could have dinner by ourselves."

"Anything to help April get through this." She kissed him on the cheek. "And to help you and April find your way back to each other."

"Think good food will win her over?"

"Couldn't hurt. That and my handsome son."

"Thanks again, Mom."

She'd had Reed's daddy grill them two juicy ribeye steaks, and she'd fixed fresh steamed vegetables and chocolate mousse, knowing April loved chocolate.

Reed watched his mom leave, then turned to check himself in the mirror over the long buffet. He wore a tuxedo—something his mother had suggested. His hair was combed and he smelled fresh and clean. "Guess I'll do."

"Oh, you'll do just fine."

He turned to find April standing at the arched door to the dining room; his breath caught in his throat as he took in the sight of her.

She wore a creamy satin sleeveless dress with a big collar that framed her slender shoulders and showed off her long neck. The dress flared out at her waist in a full-skirted halo that dropped almost to her ankles. She wore matching cream-colored shoes, and pearls on her ears and around her neck.

Reed had always loved April in her pearls.

"You'll do, too," he said, his voice husky

and intimate. "Come here and let me look at you."

She whirled into the room like a ballerina, smiling over at him. "It was my mother's. I found it in the storage closet where Flora put all her clothes."

"Pretty as a picture," he said, holding her out away from him as he looked her over. Then he leaned close and gave her a peck on the cheek. "Happy birthday, April."

Her eyes widened, first in surprise, then in a dark sadness. "It is my birthday, isn't it?"

"Yes. That's what this party is all about."

Her eyes turned misty then. "Thank you."

Reed kissed her again, then gently touched her cheek. "No tears tonight, okay?"

"Okay," she said, the one word shaky.

He tugged her toward the table. "C'mon in."

She glanced around the room. "Reed, this is so nice."

"How's Stuart?"

"He's the same. Lynette promised to call me if anything changes, good or bad."

"So we can have an hour alone, just to talk?"

She nodded, glancing back out toward the hallway. "I have to admit, I feel a little guilty, all dressed up like this, with him so sick."

Reed came around the table to pull her close. "We're right here, sugar. Right here nearby. Your daddy wants you to be happy. You can take a little time to eat and relax."

"I hope so. I'm not sure I have an appetite, but everything sure looks good."

He smiled, touched a hand to her curling bangs. "We missed the Cattle Baron's Ball. It's tonight, in Dallas."

"You could have gone—to represent the Big M."

"Not without you."

"That's so sweet."

Reed tugged her close, taking in the scent of lilies and honeysuckle that seemed to float around her. "Right now, I don't feel very sweet. I feel selfish, because I just wanted some time with you all to myself."

"At least you're honest."

"I'm trying…and I'm trying to be patient."

She pulled away and turned toward the table. "Why don't we eat this wonderful food?"

"Okay." He backed off, knowing she was still skittish. Knowing and wondering when she'd just give in and love him the way he loved her. Or let him love her the way she should be loved.

"Let's say grace," April said, then she bowed her head and thanked God for the bounty of the Big M. *"And for keeping all of us safe. Give my father some peace, the peace that he needs right now. And help Tomás and his family, Lord. We ask this in Your name."*

"Amen," Reed said. "Here you go," he told her as he adjusted her chair. "Want some mineral water?"

"Sure." She watched as he poured sparkling water from a green bottle chilling in the ice bucket. "Thanks."

He waited as she took a long drink. "Good?"

"Tingly. That hit the spot."

Reed fell for her all over again, simply because she seemed nervous and fragile. And she looked so young and pretty, just like on that night of her sixteenth birthday.

"Ever wish we could turn back the clock?" he asked.

She took up her knife and fork. "Of course. I wish I could make Daddy well, and…that Mama was here with us. I wish I could understand why death has to separate us."

Reed saw the sadness in her dark eyes. "I don't know how you handle it, knowing he's dying. I think about my parents and how much I love them. It's just hard to imagine, even when we know we'll see them all again one day."

"It is hard," she said, nibbling on her vegetables. "I haven't handled it very well. I want to blame God, you know. But I understand it's a part of life and no one's to blame. Death is just part of the journey. It's really another part of life, just in a different place."

"You're very wise to think that."

"My mother taught me to have faith, always."

"Do you have faith in me, April?"

He watched the play of emotions on her face, saw the joy, the fear, the pain, the hope. And waited for her answer.

"You've been so kind, Reed. So much a part of my life. I couldn't have made it this far without you here, helping me out. I didn't want to admit that, didn't want to look weak and helpless. But I've come to realize that turning to someone for help isn't a sign of weakness. It's a sign of strength, a sign of how much I do believe in you."

Reed leaned back in his chair. "Wow, that was some speech."

"But it wasn't what you wanted to hear?"

He threw down his fork. "You know what I want to hear, but I don't have the right to ask you that, not now, when Stuart is so sick."

April leaned forward and grabbed his hand. He saw the tears brimming in her eyes. "Are you willing to wait for me, Reed? Are you willing to give me some more time?"

Reed got up and pulled her out of her chair. "I've been waiting all my life. What's a little more time?"

Then he kissed her, to show her that he was more than willing to wait. But on his own terms. "I want you to love me again, April. I just want that—whenever you're ready."

He saw in her eyes that she did love him. He felt in her kiss that she had always loved him.

Patience. He had to learn patience. But he'd been so very patient, for so long.

April looked up at him, touching his face. "I don't deserve you."

"You deserve to be happy. You deserve...whatever can make you happy. I hope I can help in that department. I promise I'll try."

"I just need to get through this. And then, I'll decide what to do...about everything."

That wasn't exactly what he wanted to hear. "About us, you mean?"

"Yes, about us. About the ranch. Everything."

Then she kissed him again, feathering his face with little butterfly touches. "Can we break into that chocolate mousse now?"

Reed had to laugh at that. "You're trying to distract me."

"Will it work?"

"No. I can't be distracted from getting what I want. You should know that about me."

"I do. It's one of the things I love—"

"One of the things you love about me?"

"Yes."

"I guess that'll have to do for now," he said as he handed her a dessert dish full of the creamy mousse.

She smiled and grabbed a spoon. "It's a start."

The dinner ended way too soon for Reed. They'd finally settled down to small talk and laughter. He loved the way April laughed. When she was truly happy, her whole face lit up, her creamy porcelain skin glowing with an inner light.

He wanted to make her laugh for all the days of their life.

"Thank you again," she told him as they carried their plates into the kitchen. "This evening was so lovely. And it did help me to relax. It was a very thoughtful birthday present."

"Good," he said. "Let's take a stroll around the backyard before we say good-night."

She raised her dark brows. "Okay."

"Don't worry. It's just a friendly walk— to fight off the calories in that chocolate mousse."

She laughed at that. "I guess that would be smart."

He took her out by the pool. "Look at those stars."

April followed his gaze, lifting her head to the dark heavens. "A clear night, after all that rain last night."

Reed pulled her back against his chest, then wrapped his hands around hers at her side. "The good Lord always sends us signs of his beauty and his bounty, even after a bad storm."

"It was a bad night all the way around," April said, a long sigh leaving her body. "I still can't believe Tomás would be involved in such a thing."

"He's young and misguided," Reed replied, resting his chin on top of her silky curls. "And his parents have always allowed him to kinda run wild. They left things up to Flora and Horaz."

"And they tried, they really did," April added. "But Tomás isn't their responsibility, no matter how much they want to help him."

"I think things will change now. Some good should come of this bad. We've given those boys a second chance. I just hope they don't mess up again."

"I don't think Tomás will. At least he has all of us behind him." April turned to face him then. "You are a good man, Reed. You always look for the good in others, too. And you're always willing to give people another chance."

He touched his forehead to hers. "Hush, you're making me blush."

"I just want you to know—"

The ringing of the doorbell pealed through the house, stopping April in mid-sentence. "Now who could that be this late? Maybe Uncle Richard forgot his key."

She hurried inside, her skirts swishing. Reed followed her. "Hey, wait up." After last night's break-in, he didn't want her answering the door without him right there.

The bell rang again just before April opened the big door. "I'm coming." Turning to look back at Reed, she whispered, "Someone sure is impatient."

When she turned back to face the visitor, Reed heard her sharp intake of breath. Then he felt a definite chill as her body stiffened.

"Danny, what are you doing here?"

The man standing at the door had sandy-blond hair and an attitude, from what Reed could tell. Reed hated him on the spot. Something about the arrogant way the man slanted his gaze possessively over April brought out Reed's protective instincts.

And his jealousy.

"May I come in?" the man asked, waving a hand in the air. "The bugs in Texas are just as big as everything else around here."

April shot Reed a confused, shocked look. "Of course. Come in." She motioned to Reed. "Reed Garrison, meet Danny Pierson."

"Reed?" Danny's icy-blue eyes glazed over as he stared at Reed. "Well, I've certainly heard a lot about you. You and April…grew up together, right?"

"That's right," April interjected before Reed could explain how things were. She gave Reed a warning glare as she closed the door.

"And who are you?" Reed asked, shaking the hand the other man extended. After all, his mama had taught him manners. But his daddy had taught him how to fight.

And he sure smelled a good ol' fight coming on.

Apparently, so did April. "Danny is—"

"Her ex-boyfriend," Danny finished. "But I hope to change that." He put an arm around April's shoulder, then smiled over at Reed. "Know what I mean?"

"I think I do," Reed said, a slow rage burning its way through his system. Then he glanced at April and saw the distress on her face. "Maybe you should have called first. This isn't a good time. April's father is ill."

"I'm aware of that." Danny scanned them both with a puzzled look. "Is that why you're both so dressed up?"

Reed curled his fists at his side. "We were having dinner. A *private* dinner."

"Oh." Danny shrugged, tightening his grip on April. "Hope I didn't interrupt anything important. But April and I have some unfinished business."

Reed stepped forward. "I don't think—"

"Reed, it's okay," April said, coming between them. "Danny's company—Fairchild's Department Stores—is under contract with Satire. We just need to work out some of the details."

Reed glared at the other man as if he were a nasty bug. "Is *this* the problem you were telling me about?"

April nodded. "Yes. I mean, Danny and I have some problems to clear up. It's just business."

"Did you invite him here?"

"No, not really. But since he's here, I think I should talk to him."

"Yeah, man," Danny said, clearly triumphant. "We're just going to talk. About old times and a bright new future."

Reed felt the pulse throbbing in his jaw, felt the tension flaring through his head as he clenched his teeth.

"April, are you sure?"

"Yes," April said. Then she turned to Danny. "Why don't you wait in the den?" She pointed across the hall. "I'll just show Reed out."

"See you, Reed." Danny grinned, then turned to go into the other room.

April took Reed by the arm. "Can we talk?"

"About what?" he said as they went into the kitchen. "About that fancy city fellow coming here to win you back? April, I won't—"

"You won't what, Reed? Let him near me? Let him flirt with me?" Her eyes were snapping a dark fire, but Reed wasn't sure just which one of them she was mad at— the ex or him. Maybe both. "I'm a big girl, remember? I've lived out on my own for a very long time now."

He closed his eyes. "I don't need to hear the rest. You've had other relationships, same as me."

"Yes, but you've jumped to the wrong conclusion here, same as always. Danny and I are over. We've been over for a very long time."

"So what's he doing here?"

"He was in Dallas on business. When

he finally returned my calls, he asked to come here."

"And you told him he could? I can't believe that! Your father—"

"Stop it," she said, her face flushed, her eyes black with rage. "Just stop it. And leave, now. After everything…after all we talked about tonight, you still think the worst of me."

"April, I—"

"Just go, Reed. I can't take any more of this. Don't you see? No matter what we feel for each other, you will always, always think of me as the shallow little rich girl who broke your heart. You don't even believe what I've tried to explain to you. You think you know what's best for me. I can't go through that again."

Broken and baffled, Reed slowly nodded his head. "Well, neither can I."

He turned and stomped through the house to the open doors leading out to the pool. And he didn't look back.

He couldn't look back.

He'd just used up the last of his patience. There was nothing left. Nothing but an aching emptiness that was as vast and deep as the beautiful starry sky over his head.

"I guess nothing good is gonna come out of this particular situation after all, Lord," he said, his questioning prayer echoing out over the night.

When he reached his truck, he turned and looked back at the glowing lights from the house. And he felt like that teenager all over again, on the outside looking in.

Chapter Fourteen

April held her hands to her temples, massaging away the nagging headache that seemed to be coming on strong. This night had been just about perfect, but now it was going downhill very fast.

"Feeling bad?" Danny asked as she came back into the den.

April dropped her hands to stare at him. He looked every bit as handsome as she remembered him. But now she could see through all that charm. And besides, he'd ruined her night with Reed. She'd have to deal with *that* one later. Now she just wanted Danny gone. "I'm not feeling at my best, no. Danny, why did you come here?"

He shrugged and picked up a small crystal bowl from the coffee table, moving it from hand to hand. "I thought we had some business to discuss."

April grabbed the bowl before he managed to drop it. "The only business we have is this—we're over, through, finished. And you didn't have to create this little snag in the contracts between Satire and Fairchild's just to get back at me."

"Oh, you think that's what this is all about?" he asked, coming so close she could smell his expensive aftershave. That scent had at one time made her all giddy. Now she just wanted to be sick.

"Isn't it?" she asked. "I told you not to come here. My father is dying, this ranch is in a mess, and I don't need you to complicate things."

"Nothing complicated about me, babe," he said, one finger trailing down her face to her neck. "I just wanted to see you again."

"So you did plan this whole thing?"

He smiled, shifting closer. "Of course I did. The contracts are pretty standard, but I managed to find a couple of loopholes. So I used that as an excuse. That and a quick trip to Dallas. Then it made sense to swing by here and see you."

April backed away. "This is ridiculous. You're not only wasting my time, but you're using Fairchild's perks to take a side trip to Paris, Texas? Danny, not only is that risky, it's downright stupid. You could lose your job."

"I have the authority to do whatever I see fit regarding the Satire line. My employer knows what I'm doing."

"But I bet you put a really good spin on things, just as you've always done."

She turned, but he grabbed her by the wrist, twisting her back around. "Don't walk away from me, April."

"Let me go," she said, her resolve giving way to the warning moving through the pain of her headache.

"Oh, no. I didn't come all this way to be ignored."

"Danny, I don't know what you expected, but I can't help you. Not with the contracts, and certainly not with us. The contracts can't be changed without a big, ugly battle, and I'm not interested in anything you have to say regarding us."

"Without a big, ugly battle there, too, you mean?" he said, his eyes flaring a white-blue. "Is it because of *him?*"

April yanked her arm away, then rubbed the spot where he'd held her. "If you mean Reed, it has nothing to do with him. But it has everything to do with *you.* I don't feel the same about you as I once did."

"Oh, yeah, I remember. Because I'm ruthless and cutthroat and I don't play fair?"

"That and other things," she said, remembering his quick temper and his refusal to compromise on any issue at all, including her faith. "I think you just need to leave."

"Not yet," he said, coming toward her.

April turned just as he grabbed her

around the waist. He tried to kiss her, but she pushed him away. "Danny, stop it."

"Oh, don't play that game."

He tried again, but April was too quick this time. She scooted around a high-back chair. "I asked you to leave and I mean it. Do you want me to report your behavior to the CEO of Fairchild's?"

"You'd do that, just to get even?"

"I'd do that just to get rid of you."

"You know, I can stall on these contracts, hold up the entire shipment of Satire ready-to-wear."

"You go right ahead," April said, weary with all his threats. Weary to her very bones. But she had more backbone now than she'd had when they were dating. "I'd like to see you explain that to the higher-ups. Fairchild's is already in a heap of trouble. It wouldn't do to miss this chance to make a comeback. I don't think it would sit well with all those people you're trying to impress. And I know how hard you try to impress, Danny."

She saw the anger flaring in his eyes. He came at her, trying to grab her arms, but she was ready for him. April swung around and picked up the nearby cordless phone. "Just touch me again and I'll have the whole ranch down on your head."

He stepped back, hands up. "I guess I misjudged you, April. I thought you'd come begging."

"I don't beg anyone."

He stood silent, staring at her for a moment. Then he let out a defeated sigh. "Okay. I don't want a fight. I just wanted to put things right between us."

"Things will be fine if you leave now. But if you ever try to pull something like this again, Danny, I'll have to report you. And I don't want to have to do that."

He shrugged, checking the anger she could see pulsing in his jawline. "It would be your word against mine."

"Yes," she said, remembering how they'd been happy together at one time. But it had been a false happiness, and it hadn't withstood the test of time. Not the way her friendship, her love for Reed, had. Maybe God had sent Danny here for that very reason, so she could see what a real love between a man and a woman should be like, even with time and separation between them.

Why had she sent Reed away? He would have made quick work of getting rid of Danny Pierson for her. But April knew it was better this way. This was her battle, not Reed's, no matter how much Reed would want to protect her. If she couldn't stand up to Danny, she'd never be able to face Reed or anyone else again. She wanted Reed's respect and she wanted him to see that she wasn't that spoiled socialite he'd accused her of being the day she left.

She looked over at Danny, feeling nothing for him. That, and knowing that her love for Reed could be a blessing instead of a fear, gave her the courage she'd never had before. "It would be your word against mine. But I think you know which one of us people would believe. After all, you haven't exactly been discreet and tactful in how you treat people."

"I guess I haven't at that." He slumped against a chair, scowling. "And you've been a model of propriety."

His sarcasm and criticism didn't sting the way they should have. April had been through so much since the last time she'd seen him. He had no idea just how strong she'd become. But he was about to find out.

"I don't have to justify myself to you, Danny. Now, I think it's time for you to leave—"

"April!"

Lynette's frantic call from the hallway stopped April in midsentence. She whirled and hurried down the hall. "What is it?"

But when she saw Lynette's tear-streaked face, she knew. She knew.

"Is he—"

"It's bad," Lynette said, taking both of April's hands in hers. "You'd better come. I'll call Richard, too."

April gave Danny a helpless look. "I have to go."

Danny nodded, his face going pale. "I understand."

April didn't have time to make sure he left the house. She rushed to her father's room, dread coursing through the erratic pulse beating its way through her system.

Reed entered the house from the back. The dining room was dark, but a light burned from the kitchen and the long hallway. He went into the kitchen and found Flora sitting at the counter, her hands clasped in prayer.

She looked up at the sound of his steps. "Reed! It's so sad. So sad."

Reed could feel the weight of death pushing through the house. Just hours ago, he and April had laughed and talked, walked through the gardens. Then he'd gone and gotten all riled up and ruined things. Again.

He wouldn't hurt April again. And he

wouldn't allow himself to be hurt again. He'd just about decided that maybe she would never love him the way he loved her, that maybe she'd changed but he'd stayed the same. He'd been in the same holding pattern since the day she'd left. Maybe she was right in getting angry with him each time he tried to step in and save the day.

But wasn't that what being a life partner, a helpmate, was all about? Shouldn't he be the one to always be by her side and hold her up in her time of need? He was just an old-fashioned country boy who loved a so-phisticated, very modern city girl. But it wouldn't matter, if he couldn't make her love him back.

He might just have to accept that and let her be.

When Richard had told them it was near the end, Reed hadn't hesitated to come here and be nearby. Just in case she needed him.

"I know, Flora," he said now, taking the woman's withered hand in his. "It's tough.

But you and Horaz, you know you mean the world to him, and to April. She'll need you both now."

"*Sí,*" Flora replied, nodding. "Horaz is in the den with that other man. Waiting."

"What other man?"

"That stranger who showed up."

"Oh, Danny Pierson? He's still here?"

She bobbed her head again. "He said he no leave with April's father dying. He said he wanted to stay in case she need him."

"I'll take care of him," Reed said. Then he stalked across the entranceway, determined to throw that no-good out on his ear.

But the sight he saw made him stop and stare—and feel ashamed for his take-no-prisoners attitude. No wonder April had kicked him out earlier.

Horaz was talking quietly to Danny Pierson, talking and nodding his head, a gentle smile on his face. And Danny seemed to be listening. Gone was all the arrogance and the bluster Reed had witnessed on meeting the man earlier. Danny seemed intent on what Horaz was saying, his expression one of concern and respect.

Both men looked up as Reed entered the room.

"Hola," Horaz said, getting up to shake Reed's hand.

"Hey," Reed said, puzzled down to his boots. "What's going on?"

Danny stood then and extended his hand. "I'm so sorry about April's dad. Horaz was just telling me about him. He sounds like a decent man."

"He is," Reed said, wondering if this night could get any more confusing. "And what are you still doing here?"

Danny raised a hand. "Hey, now, I know I came on a little strong before, but April set me straight. I was wrong to come here, but now that I'm here, well, I can't just leave her. I have to make sure she's okay."

"Do you even care about how she feels?"

"Of course I do," Danny said, sincerity making him look a whole lot younger than

Reed had first believed. "I—I just wanted to see if there was any chance—"

"Not a chance," Reed said.

"She told me that." Danny let out a breath. "She's changed. She seemed more sure of herself."

"April has always been very self-assured."

Danny came to stand face to face with Reed. "Now that's where you're wrong. At times, she seemed very insecure to me. And she let me walk all over her. But she didn't do that tonight. Tonight she stood up to me and told me how things are. I thought I could just come in here and get her back with threats and my old condescending routine, but it didn't work this time."

Reed let that soak in, thought seriously about punching the guy, then asked, "And do you understand now? How things are?"

"I think I'm beginning to," Danny said, some of the old smugness coming out again. "It's you, man, all the way. I think it was always you. But, hey, I can't fight all that's going on here. I just didn't want to leave. Not yet."

Reed wanted to toss the man out the door, but how would that make him look? April was already steamed at him. He didn't want to make a scene, not tonight. Danny was right. April had changed, even if Reed still saw her as that beautiful sixteen-year-old socialite. She was stronger now, still determined, still beautiful, but a whole lot more courageous. Or maybe she'd been courageous all along and Reed just hadn't seen it. He'd always thought she'd been a coward for running from their love. But didn't it take courage to do what she'd done? To move across the country to a strange place and start a new life? Didn't it take courage and strength to leave everything and everyone she loved, in order to overcome her father's grief? And her own? She'd had to start over in order to become the best person she could be. But surprisingly, she'd never lost her faith in God in all that time.

Why was that so very clear to him now?

Reed suddenly realized that maybe he'd changed, too. Normally, he would have fought a cad like Danny Pierson with all his might, no questions asked. But in spite of his jumping to conclusions earlier tonight and making April mad at him all over again, Reed had shown restraint. He'd left quietly, if reluctantly.

If only he'd kept the faith, as April had done. He'd never given her the benefit of faith. He'd never actually believed in her. And that was part of the reason she hadn't turned back to him now.

"You want me to go?" Danny asked.

"Sit down," Reed told Danny. "I'm going back to check on her."

Danny sank back down in the chair then glanced over at Horaz. Horaz nodded and lowered his head, silent but sure.

Reed decided Danny was in good hands with Horaz, so he headed toward the back of the house, his footsteps sounding against the tiled floor. He dreaded going into that room, dreaded seeing April and her father. But she needed someone to be there with her. She needed someone to believe in her.

He wanted to be that someone. This time, he wouldn't let her down.

Chapter Fifteen

April stood over her father's grave, the mist of a silent rain falling in a gentle dance all around her. April didn't feel the cool mist or hear the soft rumble of thunder in the distance. She couldn't smell the sweet, clinging scent of so many flowers covered with the tears of rain. She was lost somewhere in the past.

She was remembering all the good times. She'd had a blessed life, growing up here on the Big M. She'd had parents who loved and cherished her. They'd given her the world. Her mother had taught her always to have a life of faith, always to put God first in all things, no matter how privileged their life had been. And even though she'd tried to do that, April had never understood the responsibility that came with vast wealth, or the obligations that came with a deep, abiding faith, until now.

Now, all of this belonged to her. And she didn't know if even her strong faith could sustain her.

She could feel the weight of that responsibility on her shoulders, could hear her mother's laughter, could see her father's brilliant smile.

"What am I supposed to do now, Daddy?" she asked, the chill of the spring day causing her to wrap her arms around herself. "I miss you already. I miss you so much and, now, I miss Mama all over again. I'm all alone."

"No, you're not."

She turned to find Reed standing there with a raincoat and an umbrella, his eyes washing over her in the same misty way the water was washing over the cemetery.

"We missed you back at the house," he said as he stepped forward. "Had a feeling you'd be here."

She turned back to stare down at the flower-covered grave. "I guess everyone thinks I'm incredibly rude."

"They all understand," he said as he draped the coat around her shivering body and held the umbrella over both of them.

He didn't speak again and April thanked him for that, her heart brimming with love for him and this land. If she could just let go enough to accept that love.

Finally, she cleared her throat and pushed away the tears. "Is the house still full?"

"Just the family now," Reed said, one arm holding her steady. "Summer and Autumn are doing a good job with supervising the food and the visitors. They were even nice to Danny before he left. But they were worried about you."

"I just needed some air." Then she sent

him a soft smile. "You were nice to Danny, too. Thanks for letting him stay at your house."

"It was interesting—two of your exes talking about old times."

"I guess y'all compared notes?"

"No, I'm just teasing about that. I told him he was welcome to stay as long as he didn't mention anything about your time with him, or ask me anything about you and me now. He understood and he was a perfect gentleman."

"Imagine that. I think this trip has changed him."

"It's changed all of us."

"Yes, I guess it has."

She felt the tug of his hand against the coat. "Remember that verse from Isaiah? 'The grass withers, the flowers fade, but the word of the Lord stands forever'?"

She nodded, thinking these flowers were too beautiful ever to fade. But they would. They would.

"I've always loved that particular verse."

She let out a struggling laugh. "And why are you telling me this?"

He kissed the top of her head. "Just to remind you that some things withstand the test of time. That love surpasses pain and death. I understand that you're scared about a lot of things, but God's love and grace will get us through this, April."

She laid her head on his chest, seeking the warmth and security that he offered. "I know. That's what I keep telling myself. It's just so hard to understand, to accept. We should have had a good life together, my parents and I. I wanted them to see their grandchildren, to live to be very old. I wanted so much for them. Now that will never happen."

"They will see it all, April. They'll be watching over you."

"I have a lot to think about," she said. "Too much to think about."

"Take your time. The Big M is functioning. We all know what needs to be done."

"You've been taking care of things for a

long time now, Reed. Thank you for that. And for being there the other night, when…when—"

"Shhh." He kissed her again, a soft whisper against her temple. "I'm not going anywhere."

"Uncle Richard will be a big help," she said, gaining strength with that reassurance. "I'm not so sure about Uncle James. He couldn't wait to leave today. Probably afraid Summer would light into him and her mother, the way she kept glaring at them."

"Yep." Reed became quiet again, then turned her to face him. "April, about the other night when Danny showed up—"

"Look, Reed, I was a bit stressed out that night. I mean, all that with Tomás, then Danny."

"I know. But there is no excuse for how I reacted to Danny Pierson being here. I'm sorry I jumped to the wrong conclusion. I seem to do that, where you're concerned."

"It's water under the bridge," she said. "We've been through worse."

"Yeah, like me always doubting you. I can see now why you bolted and went to New York. It wasn't just about your father's grief. It was because I was smothering and demanding, right? And I never believed in you enough to show a little faith."

April raised her head to stare over at him. "Reed, none of that matters now."

"Yes, it does. It matters more than ever. I don't want that to happen this time."

April could feel the weight pressing at her heart. "Things are different now. I'm not that young girl who clung to your every word."

"No, ma'am, you are not that. You're a woman. But you're still the only woman I want."

April pulled away, her breath catching in her throat. "I can't think about this right now. I've got so much to consider, so many things to decide."

She watched as Reed stepped back. "Okay. I guess I thought that part had been decided—that you and me belong together."

"Belonging together and *being* together

are two different things," she said. "I've got to decide what's best for my future. Do I stay here or go back to New York? I don't know."

She could tell that wasn't what he wanted to hear, but she wasn't going to fight with Reed right here over her father's grave. "Can we talk about this later?" she added.

He nodded, a gentle resolve in his eyes. "C'mon. You're freezing. Want me to drive you back to the house?"

"I did walk," she said, shaking her head. "I took off before the rain came and I just sort of wound up here."

"We could take the long way home."

She raised an eyebrow. "Oh, yeah?"

"Let's go for a long drive around town."

"That sounds nice. I'm not ready to face everyone back at the house just yet."

"Okay, then. Let's go."

Reed drove his mother's car through Paris, Texas, past the Culbertson Fountain in the historic district. "Did you know this is considered the prettiest plaza in all the state of Texas?" he asked April, hoping to make her laugh.

She did laugh. But she still sat slumped over in her corner of the car. "Well, it *is* lovely."

He drove by the old railroad depot, then on past some of the old homes lining the streets. "This rain is nice. We needed a good rain."

"Yes, I guess we did."

"I called Mom and told her we were going for a drive, so no one would worry about you."

"Thanks."

"Want to see the Market Square Mural? That's always a crowd pleaser."

"Reed, I know what Paris looks like. No need to be my tour guide."

"Sorry. Guess you do remember some of it, even if you never took that fancy convertible of yours for a spin."

"I remember all of it." She smiled over at him. "Remember that summer my mother insisted we have our picture taken in front of the Eiffel Tower—our Eiffel Tower?"

He laughed, hoping she was at last beginning to feel better. "I sure do. She made me wear a red cowboy hat just like the one up on the tower. I think my mom has a copy of that picture somewhere."

"And I had on red boots. My mother wanted to do an abstract—with the picture all black and white, except for the hats and my boots. She said that replica was truly a Texas treasure and that the red hats and boots would represent the heart of Texas and us. And she said that we didn't need Paris, France. Not when we had Paris, Texas."

"Your mother was amazing."

"Yes, she was. So talented."

"You know, I have one of her abstracts hanging in the den at my house."

"Yeah?"

"Uh-huh. When your dad decided to sell me the guest house, he gave that picture to me as a housewarming gift."

"I haven't even seen your house."

"I know. One day, I'll give you the tour."

"One day."

Reed noticed the crape myrtles blooming all over the place. Along the roadsides, the red clover and Indian paintbrush were beginning to spring up. Out in the field, the bluebonnets tipped their heads to the rain.

"It's almost summer," he said. "Lots of work to do."

April sat up and looked over at him. "Stop the car, Reed."

Concerned, he pulled the car over at a small park. "You okay?"

She bobbed her head, then turned to look at him.

"I have to go back, you know."

His heart did a quick thud, then sank down. "To New York, you mean?"

"Yes. I have to take care of some things."

"Is that your way of telling me you won't be back here?"

"I don't know," she said. The honesty in

her eyes hurt him. It was too bright, too expectant.

He turned toward her. "April, I know today was hard on you. The funeral, all the people, everything. You've got a lot of burdens to bear, and I don't want to be one of them. If you need to go back to New York, then I guess all I can do is kiss you goodbye."

"Just like that?"

"Just like that. What do you expect me to do, beg you to stay? You know I want that, but only if you want it, too."

"You'd let me go, and not condemn me or resent me?"

"I've never condemned you. I resented that we couldn't be happy together. But happiness has to come with certain sacrifices. I can see that now."

"But Reed, is it fair for you to sacrifice *your* happiness while you wait for me to decide about things?"

"I'm happy. I was happy."

"Until I came back."

He tugged her into his arms. "Listen, I

love you. I have always loved you. You can see that. Anybody with two eyes can see that. I can't hide it. But…we've both changed. I've learned to be patient, but I've also learned to be less demanding and more understanding."

"So you won't be angry when I leave again?"

"I'll be hurt, but not angry. I wish…I wish I could just sweep you up and take you home to the life I've always dreamed about us having. But that wouldn't be right. It wouldn't be fair. You had to go away once. And now it's time for you to go away again. We both knew it was coming."

She hugged him close. "I won't neglect the Big M. I promise. I won't let anything happen to the ranch."

Reed held her tight, shutting his eyes to the reality of her leaving him again. "I know you won't. And we'll all be here to help."

"You've always been right here."

"Yes, ma'am." He held back the pain. Was he crazy to hold on to such an uncertain hope? To cling to that dream of having her as his wife? "Maybe it's time for me to throw in the towel, though."

She raised her head. "What does that mean?"

"Maybe it's time for me to accept that you might not feel the same way—about us, I mean."

She touched a finger to his lips. "Don't say that. I can't keep expecting you to wait. But I don't want to lose you, either. I don't know what's wrong with me."

Reed knew what was wrong. "You've just lost your father. You're dealing with so much pain and grief. I won't push you for anything else right now. But when you're ready, I'll be here. Right here. Will you remember that, and…just call me if you need me?"

She fell back into his arms, her tears pouring out like the rain shrouding them inside the car. Reed held her as she cried, the gray of the dreary afternoon turning to the darkness of a rainswept night. He held her and accepted that he might not ever be able to hold her again.

"Hold on, I'm coming."

April ran to the ringing phone, dropping bags as she went. It was one of her co-workers from Satire, wanting to see how she was doing and if she wanted to go out to dinner with the gang. In the couple of weeks she'd been back, she'd had all sorts of invitations.

"Thanks for the offer," April said, her eyes scanning the New York skyline. "But I'm just going to stay in tonight and catch up on some work."

"That's what you tell everyone who calls here," Summer said from the doorway after April hung up. "You should get out more."

April started putting away the groceries she'd picked up around the corner. "I don't want to go out."

Autumn came out of the bathroom draped in her old terry robe, with a towel on her head. "Did I hear the phone ringing?"

"It was for April," Summer said, making a face. "She declined a fun night on the town, from what I could gather."

"I don't want to go out. End of conversation," April said, annoyed with her well-meaning but overbearing cousins.

"Have you heard from Reed?" Autumn asked as she fixed herself a cup of tea.

"No. And I don't expect to hear from Reed. Why should Reed call me? I left him. Again."

"You didn't leave *him,* technically," Summer pointed out. "You just left Texas. Again."

April turned to face her cousins. "Do y'all ever wish we could just pack up and go home?"

"I knew it," Summer said, stomping her sandal-clad foot. "You *want* to go home, don't you, sugar?"

April sank down on a high stool at the counter. "I think I've finally made up my mind. But I had a little help from a most unlikely source."

"Tell us," Autumn said, getting out two more tea bags and cups.

April pushed at her hair, tugging the silk scarf away from her throat. "Katherine fired me today."

"What?"

"Well, she fired me, then she offered me another position with Satire."

"Katherine is a strange bird," Autumn said, shrugging. "So what kind of other position?"

"Western region director of Satire ready-to-wear. I'd be based in Dallas."

Summer plopped on the couch. "As in Dallas, *Texas?*"

"Yes. That would be the one."

Autumn hopped around the counter. "That would mean you'd be near home, honey! Near—"

"Near Reed," April finished. "I'd be able to work *from* home, according to Katherine. It would involve some traveling and time spent in Dallas, but for the most part, I'd be able to work from the Big M."

Summer twisted her lips, a sign that her mind was racing. "Does Katherine know about this thing between Reed and you?"

"I told her some of it when I got back a couple of weeks ago." She shrugged. "Katherine knew something was wrong. She thought I was just depressed about Daddy, but when I started telling her, everything kind of spilled out."

"I think Katherine is compromising," Autumn said with a practical tone. "She doesn't want to see you go, so she's come up with a way to keep you and let you go home, too."

"Amazing," Summer said.

"Amazing," April repeated.

"Are you going to accept?" Autumn asked.

April sat there, her heart thudding a beat that told her at last she could have it all. "What if I do and…it's too late for Reed and me? I've held him away for so long. I was so afraid. And the funny part is, now I'm not afraid of loving him, but I *am* afraid to tell him that. Because I think I've waited *too* long."

"Oh, I don't think it will ever be too late for that, honey," Summer said. "That man is so in love with you."

"And I love him," April said, thinking the words sounded strange, being said out loud. "I love Reed."

"Well, amen," Summer shouted. "Admitting it is the first step, you know."

"The first step to what?" April asked, still scared silly.

"To being happy," Autumn finished. "Now, why don't you call Reed and tell him?"

"I can't do that yet," April said. "I have to find the courage."

"You could just surprise him and show up," Summer replied.

The thudding in April's heart changed tempo, began a new, hopeful beat. "Maybe I will."

"You ought to just call the woman," Richard said. "It's been over two weeks. Don't you worry about her?"

"Every hour on the hour," Reed admitted.

They were standing near the roping arena, watching one of the hands work with a feisty colt. It was a clear day with a powder-blue sky full of promise.

"I've talked to her, of course," Richard replied, his hands slung over the fence. "I'm kinda keeping things going until she can get back down here."

"Did she say she was coming back anytime soon?"

"I think she'll want to check on things from time to time."

"And that's why I'm not going to call her. I don't like long-distance, time-to-time relationships."

Richard let out a chuckle. "You two cut the cake, you know that? You dance all around the issue here."

"Oh, and just what is the issue here?"

"That you love that girl and she loves you."

"Then why am I here and why is she there?"

Richard leaned close. "I don't know. But you're a Texan through and through, Reed. And Texans never back down from a fight."

"I don't want to fight with her anymore."

"Then don't. Just go and get her and bring her home."

"It's not that easy."

"How can you say that when you've never even tried?"

Reed stared over at April's uncle, his thudding heart changing tempo. It begin to beat with a little more strength and confidence. "You know, you're right. I've never been to New York City."

Richard slapped him on the arm. "Well, son, I'll fire up the company jet and you can be there by morning."

"Let me just go pack an overnight bag," Reed said. "This time, instead of letting her run away from me, I'm gonna run *to* her."

"Now you're talking."

Richard was right. Maybe if he went after April, she'd finally believe in their love.

* * *

"I need you to meet me by Central Park," Summer said.

April made a face at her cell phone. "Right now?"

"As soon as you can get there. I have a nice surprise for you."

"Summer, I told you I can't do lunch today."

"Just meet me," Summer said, impatience crackling through the line. "It's a beautiful day and you need some sun. And I need to talk to you."

"Where are you?"

"Fifth Avenue and 59th Street, at the fountain."

"Okay, that's not very far. I guess I can make it."

"Good. See you."

April hung up, let out a sigh toward all the files on her desk, then grabbed her purse. Summer seemed so insistent. Wondering what her cousin needed to talk to her about and what the big surprise was,

April walked out of the building, then headed toward 59th Street. "This had better be good."

"This is going to be good," Summer told Reed just before she gave him a peck on the cheek. "You were smart to call me first, buddy. Because you know she'd just bolt again if you didn't have the element of surprise on your side."

"Are you sure?" Reed asked, glancing around the busy streets. His hotel was right up the street from April's office, but he'd called the apartment first and talked to Summer. Summer had cooked up this crazy meeting at the park. Now Reed wasn't so sure.

"Trust me," Summer said. "Now, she'll be coming from that way." She waved her hand, her bangle bracelets making a soft medley. "I'm going back to work." She started walking backwards in her high heels. "Don't mess this up, Reed."

Helpless, Reed watched her go, then glanced around the plaza and over at the hills and trees of the park. "Who knew something this big and green could be in a city?"

The fact that he was talking to himself didn't seem to bother the many people passing by. They all looked serious and businesslike, and they mostly ignored him.

So he waited, enjoying the warm sunshine and the blooming flowers and the brilliant summer-new trees.

And then he saw her.

April hurried up the street, her huge baby-blue leather tote bag slung over her arm, her short hair wafting out around her face. She wore a floral print dress with tight, elbow length sleeves and a full skirt that hit just below her knees. And she had on those infernal tall sandals like Summer had been wearing.

She looked so fresh and pretty, Reed had to glance around to make sure he wasn't dreaming.

He waited, watching as she looked toward the park. Watching as her expression changed from purposeful to surprised...to confused...to happy.

Maybe Summer was right. The element of surprise seemed to be working.

"Reed?" she said as she hurried across the intersection separating them. "How—"

"Don't ask," he said as he pulled her into his arms. "Just don't ask."

She didn't. She hugged him tight. "Can I ask *why*, then?"

"Because I love you," he said as he held her away. "Because I decided it was time for me to do the running." He kissed her forehead. "I've never gone chasing after a woman, and since you're the only woman I've ever wanted...well, here I am."

"You came for me." It was a statement filled with wonder and endearment. "You came here, for me?"

"Yes, ma'am. Why else would I be standing in the middle of Manhattan in the middle of May?"

"I was coming back, you know."

"Really, now?"

"Yes. I have a new job, in Dallas. I can work from home."

"And where would home be?"

"The Big M, with you."

"So I could have spared myself this trip to the Big Apple?"

"Oh, no. Seeing you here, well, that seals the deal. Now I know you really do love me."

"You doubted that?"

"No, but you doubted me. You coming here, I think it means you don't doubt me anymore."

"No, I don't."

"Good, because I'm not afraid anymore. I love you," she said.

Reed's heart beat faster with each impatient car horn, with each tread of feet against asphalt. "I love you, too."

"Want to go home now?"

"Not just yet," he said, holding her face in his hands.

"I want to see the rest of this big park. And your city."

"I'll be glad to show it to you. And then we can go home. Together."

"Together," he said. He kissed her, the certain hope of their love coloring his world with blessings and thankfulness.

* * * * *

*Be sure to pick up the next book in
Lenora Worth's
TEXAS HEARTS miniseries,
A PERFECT LOVE,
available December 2005.*

Dear Reader,

Death is never easy to accept, but it is a part of life. As Christians, we are taught that this life is just a part of eternity. We know that a better life is still to come. But still, we weep when we lose a loved one. So we have to keep the faith and hold fast to that certain hope that will bring us eternal life.

April had to learn this lesson as she watched her father dying. She also had to learn that sometimes the things we fear the most are the very things that we need the most. She needed Reed's love, but she was afraid to embrace that love. She didn't want to be hurt. Reed was steadfast and strong, but he wanted her on his own terms. Together, they had to move toward a faith of things hoped for. They found that hope in their love for each other.

My hope for you is that your faith will always be strong enough to get you through the worst of times, and that it will bring you comfort and strength in all things.

Until the next time, may the angels watch over you always.

Lenora Worth

Love Inspired
SUSPENSE
RIVETING INSPIRATIONAL ROMANCE

Die Before Nightfall
BY SHIRLEE McCoy

A thirty-five-year-old mystery of tragic love becomes a very modern-day threat for nurse Raven Stevenson and her elderly charge's nephew Shane Montgomery.

"A haunting tale of intrigue and twisted motives."
—Christy Award winner Hannah Alexander

Available at your favorite retail outlet.
Only from Steeple Hill Books!

Steeple Hill•

Love Inspired

SUSPENSE

RIVETING INSPIRATIONAL ROMANCE

Suspicion
of Guilt

by **Tracey V. Bateman**

The Mahoney Sisters

Someone wants Denni Mahoney's home for troubled young
women shut down, but could the threat be coming from inside?

"One of the most talented new storytellers
in Christian fiction."
—CBA bestselling author Karen Kingsbury

Available at your favorite retail outlet.
Only from Steeple Hill Books!

Steeple
Hill®

SILHOUETTE *Romance*®

Escape to a place where a kiss is still a kiss...

Feel the breathless connection...

*Fall in love as though it were
the very first time...*

Experience the power of love!

Come to where favorite authors—such as

Diana Palmer, Stella Bagwell, Marie Ferrarella

*and many more—deliver modern fairy tale
romances and genuine emotion,
time after time after time....*

*Silhouette Romance—
from today to forever.*

Silhouette®

Live the possibilities